THE ADIRONDACK PRINCESS

THE ADIRONDACK PRINCESS

An Historical Novel

by

Doris E. Schuyler

SECOND PRINTING

Printed in The United States of America
by Worden Press
Brookfield, N.Y. 13314

© Copyright 1982
by
Doris E. Schuyler
All rights reserved

Library of Congress Catalog Number 82-83891

ISBN NO. 0-914821-00-8

Dedication

To William R. Schuyler, Sr.
whose patience in transcribing my handwritten manuscript and hours of typing made all this possible.

Contents

I	Escaping the fire
II	The old squaw
III	Friends of foes?
IV	Ebony
V	The proposal
VI	A prisoner
VII	Spring, and a wedding
VIII	A new home - a new way of life
IX	A pet - brings remembering
X	The search for the river
XI	A gift from the valley
XII	Death and decision
XIII	Another spring
XIV	A surprise
XV	A new venture
XVI	The canal
XVII	The Inn
XVIII	The letter
XIX	The new arrivals

Preface

This is a story of a young girl who, in her struggle to escape tragedy, finds love and friendship in the Adirondack Mountains.

Although a fictitious tale, it might easily have happened. It is also a story of the American Indians who were not savages, but wise and industrious human beings.

R. G.

THE ADIRONDACK PRINCESS

Chapter I
1785 - Upper Mohawk Valley
South of Rome, N.Y.

Emmie's knowledge of her body was very vague. She knew that men and women married, and that women bore children, but the words "human anatomy" were words with which she was not at all familiar. What she did know was that at this very moment she hurt all over — her feet were swollen and blistered, her arms were scratched and bleeding, her back and left ankle shrieked out at her with every step to stop, and she ached with every movement. But she knew that she must forge on. She had been walking, sometimes running, for several hours now. She had no idea where she was going or even in what direction she had started out.

Everything had happened so quickly. She and Ma had been eating breakfast like most any other morning, since Papa and the boys had gone off down the river to sell the pelts they had collected all winter with their trap lines. They had followed the same procedure each spring for as long as Emmie could remember. The few weeks that they were away was a lonely, but pleasant time for Emmie and Ma.

There was the cattle to look after, and daily chores to do, and a great many of these days were spent in restful chatting and doing handwork. Papa had clipped the wool from the sheep before they left, and she and Ma had been leisurely washing and carding the wool. The weather had been real warm for early spring, and the drying had come along just fine. Ma had promised her that if there was any extra wool, she would dye it red and Emmie could knit herself a sweater. She had learned to knit last winter after Papa had whittled her a pair of lovely maple needles, and she was anxious about the wool drying. Ma knew of her anxiety and had gone to the rocks at the back of the barn, where the wool was drying, when Emmie had heard her screams. Everything then happened so quickly that Emmie hadn't had time to even think about what had happened, or what she was doing, or where she was going.

Emmie had run to investigate the screams and was confronted with a barrage of wild animals stampeding toward the barns, followed by a great wall of flames, licking at their heels. Her body stiffened and her face paled with horror at the scene. It was too late to save Ma, and without even thinking, Emmie ran for the little cave by the river bank. Once safely inside, she had sat for what seemed hours, waiting for the noise of the animals and the fire to subside. She had waited all day and night, and when the sun crested over the water's edge, she had started out. She had never been alone before in her life, and now she was alone and lost. All she had eaten since yesterday's breakfast was some early blossoms she had found along the brook, but that was hours ago, and her hunger pangs were so strong that she was sure she could not continue.

Just as the last ounces of strength ebbed from her body, she came upon a small pit at the foot of a giant pine tree. She crawled in and pulled some boughs over her, and was instantly asleep. She slept for many hours, awakening only after the sun was high above the horizon. As she stood and stretched and looked around her, she was surprised to find that her yesterday's aches and pains were nearly all gone. Dried blood covered her bare arms, and as she felt her face, she knew that her face was in the same condition. She climbed a nearby knoll and looked back upon the trail that she had left behind her. From the cave at the river's edge, she had swum across the river and was now on the north side, well toward the foothills of the great mountains.

The fire and the animals had been stopped by the river, but as far as she could see, the fields and forests on the south side of the river were green and bursting with buds of spring. Only a slim, silver ribbon of smoke beyond the bend was the only visable evidence that there had been a fire. Her heart wept for Ma and all the animals that had perished, but her eyes shed no tears. She was utterly and absolutely stunned. What would she do, and where would she go? Papa and the boys wouldn't be back for at least two weeks, and she had to find a place of shelter before then. What would they think and do when they returned and found nothing but ashes? Would they bother to even look for her? Her heart hoped they would, but most probably, her mind told her, they would assume that she and Ma had both died in the catastrophe.

She walked but a few yards and found a small sparkling brook, and knelt to wash her wounds. She hadn't bothered to disrobe, the water looked so refreshing that she stepped from the bank right into the water, fully clothed. She sat down and let the cool, clean water bubble over her for many minutes before taking the hem of her skirt to rub away the dried blood. She was very engrossed in her bathing and did not hear anyone approach the creek's bank. Even so, she did not feel startled when she finally felt that someone was watching her. He was tall, almost as tall as her brother Lum, and his body was lean, and she could tell from his muscled arms and legs that he was very strong. And from the single feather in his head band, she knew him to be a young brave, not yet a warrior or with a squaw.

He lay down his bow and arrows, and stepped into the water beside her, and began to gently splash her arms and face. No words passed between them, but the gentleness with which he touched her made her unafraid. He cupped his hands together and let the cool water trickle between his fingers and run down over her like a gentle rain shower. He ran his long slim fingers through her golden hair, and pulled out the briers and twigs ever so gently. He took her hands in his and pulled her to her feet, and as they stepped up on the bank together, the water oozed from her boots, making a squishy sound at which he smiled broadly, showing a row of even, white teeth.

Emmie had never been this close to an Indian before. In fact, she had never even been on the north side of the river before. Papa and her brothers had told many tales of the red-skinned people; of how they cut off the top of your head, just to hang on their belts; of how they stole horses and burned and plundered. She could not now understand why she was walking so willingly along beside this young brave. She felt that she was a young brave too, but if that were so, who was he?

Chapter II

Emmie and the young brave had walked but a seemingly short distance when they came upon a great circle of tepees, in the center of which, great hustle and bustle was being created by women in leather and beaded garments, turning a large spit over an open fire. Emmie could see that a whole animal, perhaps a deer, was being roasted. The young man took her hand and led her to who (Emmie thought) must be the oldest person in the whole world. Her face was a cavern of wrinkles, her skin dried to nearly a parchment texture from the many years of exposure to the sun and wind and freezing cold. Among all this age and seeming despair, her eyes shone like great lights, piercing Emmie's thoughts and going completely through her body; holding her as if hypnotized — immobile — unable to move, and even making it hard for her to breathe.

The young man offered Emmie's hand to the elderly squaw, and spoke rapidly in a language Emmie had never before heard. From his gestures, she knew instinctively that all the words were about her. The withered red hand reached out and took her hand from his, and the softness of it startled Emmie. The old squaw gently led her to a large tepee at the outer edge of the circle, and as she stopped to lift the flap and enter, she still held tightly to Emmie's hand, who followed with no resistance into the cavernous interior. The old woman motioned her to a sheaf of boughs, covered with animal hides, and so Emmie sat upon this bed-like bench.

The woman had now released her hand and was busying herself among many clay pots, finally selecting one she approached Emmie and quickly began rubbing a heavy, dark, grease-like substance over her aching, scratched arms and face. This accomplished, she removed Emmie's boots, and upon seeing the condition of her feet, left, to return with a jar of hot, hot water. She gently bathed her feet and then applied the same greasy substance to them. Emmie felt immediate comfort and reclined on the sweet-smelling boughs and soon dropped off into a deep sleep.

When she awoke, complete darkness surrounded

her, both inside and outside the great tepee. There was a small pile of glowing embers in the center of the tepee, and after Emmie had been awake for a few moments and her sight had acclimated to the darkness, she could see a thin thread of white smoke rise from the embers, which reached straight upward to the small point where the supporting strays met and left a small opening. The silver thread of smoke seemed to mesmerize her and she did not realize that the old squaw was with her until she was handed a bowl. The bowl was very hot to touch, and a delicious aroma of corn and maple sugar arose from it. Emmie, using a crude spoon in the bowl, ate ravishingly of the mush. She suddenly realized that it had been many, many hours (amounting to almost five days) since she and Ma had shared the leisurely breakfast before the tragedy had consumed all that she knew of the world.

Of course, Papa and the boys had not been there, but thoughts of them now made them seem very, very far away. When she finished eating, the bowl was as clean as if washed, and she felt warm all over. While she had been asleep, a soft, subtle, almost weightless robe had been placed over her. She now drew this robe around her and looked up into the solemn face of the old squaw. The features of the face were set in a maze of wrinkles, and the mouth seemed never to smile, but the eyes smiled at her, and they no longer seemed like piercing lights as they had earlier, when she had first been given into her care by the young brave.

Emmie felt warm and comfortable, her aches and pains seemed to have vanished. She felt refreshed and able to go on. She had no idea of where she was, nor in what direction she should go, but she felt that she should not impose on these new-found friends any longer. What she did not realize was that she had slept for three days and three nights, having been much more exhausted than she had imagined or felt as she lay on the soft boughs. Her thoughts rambled, remembering the fire and Ma's screams, the stampede of the animals and her escape in the little cave. Yet, through all this, she had not had a moment to be afraid, and as her mind and body took that moment now, her body shook with great tremors of fear, and she opened her mouth to scream, but no sounds came.

The old squaw was watching all this from her pad in the shadows on the opposite side of the fire. She hesitated to go to Emmie, but when the tremors became so great as to shake Emmie's body from the pelt to the dirt floor, the old squaw stood and quietly stepped around the fire and picked up the small body and cradled her until the shaking stopped. Emmie felt comfortable with the arms of the old squaw about her. More than comfortable — safe. After several minutes the old sqauw gently released her and laid her back upon the boughs, and quietly disappeared through the narrow opening in the tepee.

In a very few minutes she returned with a bowl of steaming, sweet-smelling, very hot broth, which she carefully spooned for Emmie. It tasted so very good that Emmie was tempted to reach for the bowl and drink it all down at once, but being slightly in awe of the old woman's treatment, she restrained herself and accepted spoonful after spoonful until the bowl was empty. After which, she lay back down and quickly returned to sleep.

When she next awoke, she was alone, and through

the narrow slit in the tepee she could see bright sunlight, and so knew that yet another day had dawned. She sat up and stretched her arms, and they felt stiff, but painless. Next, she tried standing, and although she found that her feet, wrapped as they were, proved to be quite clumsy, she felt no pain. After completely stretching her whole body and peering about to ascertain that she was absolutely alone, she knelt to pray. Ma had taught her that not only being thankful, but thanking the Lord was a very important part of life in this world. And so, she knelt beside the soft pad of boughs that had been her bed for these many past days, and thanked the Lord for sparing her life, for the young brave who had brought her here, and for the old woman who had nursed her wounds, and had, Emmie prayed, under God's guidance, restored her health. As she rose, weak and exhausted from the prayer session, the old woman appeared in the opening, looked inquiringly at her, and turned and shuffled away. Emmie sat back down, wondering what she should do, then the old lady returned with more steaming broth. This time she carefully handed the bowl to Emmie and shuffled away again. Emmie drank slowly savoring every swallow. She had never tasted anything quite like this before. It had a fishy taste, but was watery thin, and was flavored with herbs that Emmie did not recognize.

Chapter III

Emmie had not much time to consider flavors, for as she drank the last drops from the bowl, the old lady reappeared, this time with a dress-like garment of soft, supple deerskin, and moccasins of the same soft leather. Since neither knew the other's language, they used hand motions, and it was soon apparent that the clothes were for Emmie, to replace those that she wore, which hung in shreds, barely covering her body.

Stronger from the broth, Emmie stood and removed the tattered rags which were once her clothes; a skirt that Ma had made for her 16th birthday, and a shirtwaist that once had tiny white buttons all the way down the front; buttons that Papa had brought back from one of his trading trips down the great river. Many of the buttons were now missing, having been torn off by the briers that had torn the material, and her own flesh. Emmie hesitated when all that covered her body were her camisole and drawers, but the old squaw motioned her on, and so she shortly stood before the Indian, her body absolutely bare. Her body was inspected for cuts and bruises, and then she was allowed to put on the dress. It felt warm and soft against her bare skin, and Emmie felt comfortable at once. Her right foot slipped into the moccasin easily, but the swelling that remained in her left foot would not allow her to put on the left one. The old squaw then knelt down and wrapped her foot and leg with strips of soft skins, binding it tightly so that Emmie felt no pain when she had finished the binding. She stood and went to the slit opening. The young brave who had brought her here many days ago stepped in, and smiling at her, he swooped her up in his arms and carried her out into the sunshine. He walked directly to a hammock-like affair that had been set up, supposedly just for her. He lowered her gently into the hammock and then stood, sentry-like, at her side. Emmie lay, wondering what in the world was going to happen to her. Her eyes were unaccustomed to the bright sunlight, and as she squinted, trying to see about her, she found herself surrounded with many, many red-skins, all looking — really staring — at her. Her heart, she felt, did a flip-flop in her chest. The young brave stood tall — arms crossed, at the foot of her hammock, and it was soon evident to Emmie that he was showing her off to his people. For the very first time since she had been here, she was scared, so very scared that her breath seemed to come in great gasps, and the pain of the breathing wracked her whole body. She tried to raise up, thinking perhaps, she could somehow flee. But what strength she had gained under the old squaw's nursing, seemed to have left her now, and she fell back against the hammock and began to cry — great wrenching sobs. Emmie had never been one to cry when she was hurt, but Ma was not there to comfort her, or Papa and the boys to protect her, and surrounded with all these strange people, she felt very alone.

As her sobbing increased, the young brave gathered her in his arms and returned her to the old squaw's tepee. He placed her on the bed of soft boughs and left her alone. When her sight was accustomed to the dimness of the interior, and she had ascertained once again that she was all alone, she got off the bed with much pain and knelt on her knees beside it and prayed. Her God was the only one left in her life that she could talk to, and talk, she did. She pleaded and begged God to send her a sign that she was safe. She fell into a deep sleep, exhausted from all the excitement of the day, and when she awoke, several hours later, she felt cramped, and her ankle was causing her much pain. Even so, she hobbled to the slit entrance and peered out. It was at this moment, as Emmie peered out into the night and her eyes fell on the slim slice of moon, that she realized how very long she had been here. The moon had been complete when she had escaped from the cave, and swum across the river, and now it was nearly time for the new moon. She had been here a whole month. Papa and the boys would have returned and found the ashes that had been their happy home. Would they even bother to search for her, or assume that all — even she and Ma — had been lost?

The ritual of the young brave carrying her to the hammock in the sun continued for many days, with the younger maidens gathering about her, even venturing to touch her. Patting her hands and stroking her long, blond hair. She soon came to realize that they thought of her as some sort of princess. Her ankle was much better, and she was now allowed to walk about and watch everyone busy at their tasks. Emmie walked alone, but the young brave was never far behind her.

Chapter IV

One day, shortly after her recovery, Emmie sat on a crude log bench and tried to communicate with the brave. Emmie crossed her arms over her breasts, slid her hands down the sides of her body, and as she did so, she repeated her name many times. Finally, she put both hands over her heart, and again repeated, "Emmie." The young brave slowly repeated the name after her, and following Emmie's method, told her his name was a name that Emmie was sure had great meaning in the Indian language. But even with much tongue twisting, she could not seem to pronounce it. Many thoughts quickly flashed through her mind, and although he was not a great physician as the Disciple Luke had been, he had brought her to his tribal medical leader, and so, at that moment, decided she would call him Luke. He smiled at this name she had chosen for him, and repeated it many times, combining it with hers, saying over and over, "Luke and Emmie." Emmie soon learned that knowing each other's name was a very small part of what they must learn about each other.

She was treated like a princess by the Indians. The women never seemed to tire of admiring her pale skin and hair, and even after her ankle was completely healed, she was not allowed to join in and help with any of the daily chores that the women performed. Although she knew that she could not leave the little village, she was allowed to roam freely about the compound.

She especially enjoyed the ponies. "Ponies," because that is what Luke called them. They were really small horses that the Indians had caught and tamed, or that they had traded with other tribes for. Emmie was particularly fond of one which was jet black. Her mother had told her a story long ago, about a boy and his horse. The horse was black, and he had called him Ebony, because he glistened so very much like the jewel-like stone, and so Emmie made friends with the animal, and she called him Ebony.

One day, when she thought she was quite alone, out by the corral, she took a halter from the fence post where many were hanging, and slipped it over Ebony's head. He stood very still, almost as if at attention, and without much thought as to what she was doing, she swung her body upward and onto the horse's back. Amost immediately, several of the braves were at the corral gate. Her heart seemed to stop beating as she looked at the solemn faces. However, unconcernedley she patted the horse's rump, and he pranced, as if on parade, around the enclosure. Emmie had no way of knowing that only the males of the Indians rode the horses. But not one of them made a move toward her. She allowed the horse to circle many times before she dismounted and removed his halter, and replaced it on the post where she had found it.

Sometime later, when she found Luke skinning a deer, she took his hand and led him to the edge of the brook that bubbled its way along the outskirts of the village. He had shown her this spot when her ankle had first been well enough for her walk on, and they had spent many hours here. There was a small, sandy cove, and they both had learned to communicate by drawing pictures in the sand. Emmie picked up a twig and soon had drawn herself upon Ebony. He quickly rubbed her image out and drew himself upon the horse's back. Emmie erased him and replaced herself. This they did several times until he finally left Emmie's figure upon the horse, and so she now knew that the horse was hers.

It wasn't long before she had picked up several words from listening and putting together words and actions. She had been with the Indians six moons now, and all the squaws in the village were very busy harvesting and preparing for fall and winter. Corn was being shucked and dried, and roots were dug and hung to dry on all the fences, and racks about the compound. Berries were spread on what Emmie thought were great reed trays that the women had woven of reeds or grass, and as they dried they were stored in baskets, also woven of reeds by the women. The men had hunted and brought back all sorts of game. Bear, deer and moose, and then smaller animals such as rabbits, raccoons and squirrels. These were skinned and the meat stripped and dried, some in the sun, and some smoked over the ever-burning fire.

The children not old enough to help with other regular chores, fished in nearby brooks and creeks, and their catch, which, when not needed for daily food, was also smoked and dried, and stored for the long winter when they would be more needed and appreciated.

Emmie watched with eagerness as the young girls were taught to prepare the winter stores, and with envy when they were taught leather work. The boys made needles from bones, and the girls, even the very young, soon became very adept in their use. The boys also made knives from bone and flint stones, which they used skillfully in preparing the hides for the women to use in the making of clothes and moccasins. Small skins were pieced together, and parka-like garments were made in all sizes to protect them against the expected cold and snow. Emmie noted the absence of metal tools. Only a few of the older braves had steel knives — no doubt taken from the bodies of fallen warriors. These, they prized very highly, using them only when their bone and flint knives seemed utterly inadequate.

Chapter V

It was a warm, sunny day in late fall and Luke had taken Emmie for a longer walk than usual. They went beyond their beach cove, down stream, beyond any points where Emmie had been allowed to venture by herself. As they stopped to rest and throw pebbles in the brook, Emmie thought for the first time in many days about Pa and the boys. She wondered what they had thought when they returned to find everything they had worked so hard for, gone. She wondered if they had started anew, and if they had looked for her.

Surely, they had found Ma's body, and not a trace of her. Emmie was deep in thought when Luke took her hand and looked solemnly in her eyes. His look brought her back to reality, and the reality that that part of her life was gone forever. Surely, if she were going to be found, someone would have come by now. She had seen no other white person since Luke had found her and brought her to the camp. And so, when he drew her a picture in the sand of herself and him together — hand in hand — she took his hand in hers and smiled and slowly nodded her head in an affirmative reply.

Luke picked her up and swung her around many times, elated with her reply. When he put her down, she quickly knelt, and taking great pains, drew and drew on the sands until she had made a picture of a tepee, a campfire and a squaw. This, she drew a line through, and then drew a small log house and barn, with a fence around it, and a field with a man and a plow. She pointed first to herself and then to him, and then drew a large circle around the little farm. He looked very puzzled, but with pictures and hand motions, and with the few words they could both understand, she finally made him know that she would be his wife, but not his squaw.

They would have a place of their own. She could not share him with all the others, and she could not live in the compound as they did now. He slowly wiped out the picture, and stood and pulled her to her feet, and they started back toward the camp. She could not tell from his facial expressions how he felt about what she had communicated, or what he would do about it. After all, he had lived all his life in a compound with his people and knew no other way of life. Nevertheless, she felt that she must take this stand or her whole life and the dreams of a home and family that she had cherished since childhood would be lost. The Indians had all seemed to hold her in some sort of reverence. They did not allow her to work or help in any way. They had been friendly and thoughtful in giving her her horse when no other female was allowed one, and so, perhaps. they would agree to this plan. And if they didn't, she would try to escape — how, she had no idea. She was so closely watched over at all times, but sometime she felt she would find herself unguarded, and dash off, she knew not where, but on Ebony. She had felt for sometime that he would know the way to the great river and to freedom.

Chapter VI

Once back in the compound, Luke left Emmie at the tepee of the old squaw, and after a short conversation, he strode away as if irritated, and left Emmie alone with the old lday, whom Emmie had come to think of as the grandmother she had never known. She immediately took Emmie's arm and quickly ushered her inside the tent and left, lacing the flap behind her. She returned, much later, with food, setting the bowl in front of Emmie without a word, and again left, lacing the flap behind her. Emmie became very frightened, not being allowed to the campfire and evening meal. They had never done this to her since her ankle was well enough for her to hobble on, she had joined the others for their evening meal, and had been allowed to sit by the open fire with the others until the Chief retired. Why were they doing this to her now? Her mind was boggled with many thoughts and reasons, and all the awful tales she had heard as a child about the red-skinned people flashed through her mind. She had never (since the first day in the hammock) felt like this and she had never felt so helpless as she did now, even when the fire had swept down on her and she had fled to the river. Now she was literally locked in. Why had Luke done this to her? She had promised to marry him, but she had also wanted a home of her own like Ma and Papa had had. Was that so very wrong? Tears rolled down her cheeks, and she put her head down on the soft boughs and sobbed. She sobbed until her strength was spent and there was no energy or will left within her. In this sad and exhausted state she finally slipped into a deep sleep.

It was dawn when she finally roused herself from the boughs, but when she was fully awake, and her eyes were accustomed to the dimness, the only light was from the flickering fire, now nearly spent. She saw that the old squaw was sitting on the other side of the fire pit, just watching her. Emmie offered a weak smile, but the old lady did not move, and so Emmie lay back down on the boughs as there seemed to be nothing to do but wait and hope. Hope that Luke would come and all would be all right.

Emmie lost track of the days that she was a

prisoner of the old squaw, but she knew from the winds and the cold air that blew through the laced flap that cold weather was rapidly approaching, and that any time now, snow would fall, and then, of course, it would be even more impossible to escape, should the opportunity present itself. Emmie never had even tried to look between the lacing, as fear gripped her heart each time she even walked around the tent, the old woman's eyes never ceased following her.

She knew, one morning as she awoke, that the snows had come at last, and that the tepee would now, if they had not decided to do away with her, be her prison for the long winter. She often wondered what had happened to Luke. Many different squaws, and even a brave, would bring their food to them, but never Luke. She resigned herself to believing that he had deserted her, either by force or by his own free will. She thought of Ebony too, and wondered if he missed her, and who was caring for him now. The winter was neither long nor hard that year. There were some hard storms, and many days the winds blew with such force that it seemed to Emmie that the tepee must surely give way to the elements, but it was very secure, and held together very well.

Chapter VII

Spring burst forth upon the little compound as a flower bursts forth from its bud. Suddenly, one day, the winter was over. Almost as suddenly, there seemed to Emmie, to be a great commotion in the yard beyond her prison. Great preparations were being made. Some sort of festivity was about to take place, and Emmie wished longingly that she could be a part of it. There was still no indication to her about her fate, but she no longer was frightened. She had prayed long and hard to the God that Ma had taught her about, and had reconciled herself to whatever fate was to be hers. She did pray also that Luke was safe. She had meant no harm to him when she had laid her plans of a home of their own before him. She hoped fervently that no harm had come to him.

The weather, from what Emmie could tell from inside the tepee, grew rapidly warmer, and she did so wish that she could run to the creek and bathe in the warm spring waters. It was in the second week of spring that several of the younger squaws appeared at the flap of the tepee early one morning. They seemed laden with heavy bundles of skins, but as the old squaw let them in, Emmie could see that they were not ordinary skins. There was a dress made of the palest deerskin, the skin so soft and fine that it almost seemed weightless. At the hemline there was a deep fringe, and the sleeves were adorned with the same deep fringe. Around the neck and down the front the decorations were made of beads, laboriously sewn into the intricate patterns. There was a shawl-like wrap, and moccasins of the same pale, weightless, skins. A narrow headband, with the same beadwork, completed the contents of the bundles. Each of the young squaws knelt before Emmie and presented her with one of the gifts until she was dressed in the complete regalia. The girls had learned her name, and now repeated in unison, "Emmie and Luke."

Emmie was overcome. She quickly understood what the gifts were for. All through the winter, when these people had virtually kept her prisoner, they had been preparing for the wedding of herself and their most handsome brave. Realizing this, great tears welled up in her eyes, and she struggled to keep them concealed. She must not let them see her weep. The tears were of joy and relief, but she was the only one who would understand. It was then that she realized that they truly believed her to be some sort of princess, and surely princesses didn't cry.

With motions of hands and arms, Emmie made known to the old squaw that she wanted some warm water, and very shortly the largest wooden vessel that she had ever seen was brought to the tepee and filled from several clay pots with warm water. After the old squaw had tightly closed the flap, Emmie slowly disrobed and sat naked in the great bowl. She splashed about for a few minutes, savoring the feel of the warm water on her body, and then she laid her head back on the rim and relaxed for several more minutes. Finally, feeling refreshed and clean, she stepped out and over to the smouldering ash pit and warmed herself until she was dry. With all this accomplished, she took from the pocket of her old, tattered skirt, a crude wooden comb that Papa had made for her many moons ago, and worked at straightening her hair, and at last, under the scrutinizing gaze of the old squaw, dressed herself in the fine gifts the young squaws had earlier brought to her. Finally, she stood before the old lady, completely dressed in the full, splendid regalia of an Indian bride. Having been inside so long with only the glow from the campfire for light, it took Emmie sometime to become accustomed to the late afternoon sun. She had been led outside by the old squaw and had been given a log stool to sit upon. All the members of the compound seemed to have gathered around the great fire that had been built in the middle of the central yard, and when Emmie was seated, the ceremony began. When her eyes were accustomed to the light, she could make out Luke on the opposite side of the fire. Several feathers had been added to his headband, meaning, Emmie knew, that he had hunted well that winter, and was now able to provide for a family.

There were chants and dancing and a great many speeches, all seeming to go on at the same time. A sudden hush came over the whole yard as the Chief appeared in what Emmie knew to be his full dress regalia. He went directly to Luke and spoke for many minutes, and then Luke rose, and with the Chief, came to where Emmie sat. She smiled long and lovingly at him, and he returned her smile. The pleasure of the occasion beamed from his bright eyes. The Chief grasped Emmie's hand and drew her to a standing position, and placed her hand in Luke's. His voice seemed as a roar in her ears as he spoke for several minutes, and then stepped back, leaving them alone, hand in hand. Everyone immediately leaped up and ran to them, forming a circle about them, and danced and sang for what seemed to Emmie, an eternity.

When the dancing and songs finally ended, they were led to a table heaped bountifully with food. Roasted meat, fresh fish, dried fruit and berries, fresh corn bread dipped in honey, and much more. Everyone immediately started to eat, and soon most of the food had been devoured. Emmie tried to eat — she was actually hungry — but the full meaning of the day's activities were beginning to take its toll, and she found herself only able to nibble a few crumbs of the bread. When the food was finally gone, and the squaws were wending their way back to their own tepees, the men gathered and shared a peace pipe together. Emmie took these few moments to go back to the old squaw's tepee and gather up her few meager possessions. The ripped blouse and torn skirt, and her undergarments. She found that these things had all been laundered and lay in a neat pile near her mat. She also found new garments like the Indians wore. There was a dress, and moccasins and leggings and a parka. These things were not as fancy as the ones she now wore, but were soft and comfortable, and, she knew, meant for everyday use. These, she quickly gathered up and made into a bundle, and then went to the flap of the tepee and waited for Luke to come for her. A young brave that Emmie did not recognize brought Luke's pony and Ebony to them. He helped her mount, and then after a quick wave to the Chief, they were off.

As they rode from the camp, the sun was setting, and Emmie wondered where they could be going, as darkness would soon envelope them. They rode on for several miles along the bubbling brook, and when finally Luke pulled his pony to a stop, they were in a stand of pines that was just east of the brook. Luke helped her down from Ebony, and led the horses to the brook, where they drank and ate ravishingly of the fresh grasses. When they had had their fill, he tethered them to a pine, not far from where Emmie stood. He quickly gathered twigs and branches and made a fire. Emmie was glad to have him do this, as the spring evening air had a decided chill, and although she had thrown the shawl about her shoulders, she still felt the spring chill reach her bones.

   The sparks soon sprang to life, and the flames danced in the air, making eerie shadows everywhere she glanced. Luke was busy with his knapsack, and soon produced some dried fish, bread and fruit, which they chewed on as they sat absorbing the heat from the fire. They gathered a great pile of soft pine needles and spent their first night together in the shadowy forest, with the stars shining brightly on them. Emmie felt secure and unafraid in the crook of his strong arm, and was soon sleeping peacefully. Luke did not drop off to sleep so fast. He lay there, looking down upon the princess he had found alone and hurt in the woods so long ago, and who that very afternoon had been made his wife. He wondered if she would be surprised and happy about what he had in store for her tomorrow. With these thoughts and wonderments on his mind, he finally fell into a deep sleep.

Chapter VIII

The morning dawned bright and warm, and after a quick breakfast of dried fruit and cold corn bread, they were on their way again. The horses were rested and fresh and ready for the journey. They had ridden, for what seemed to Emmie, many hours. The sun was now high in the sky. She wondered why Luke didn't suggest they stop and rest. But he only smiled at her each time she chose to glance at him, and forged ahead. The sun had reached its peak and was starting downward when the small cabin appeared before them.

It was a small cabin, and at first appeared to have no windows, but as they drew closer, Emmie could make out an opening about halfway up one side, over which a skin had been hung. There was also a skin hung over the doorway opening, and a crude fence surrounded the whole clearing. Emmie looked from the cabin to Luke and quickly back to the cabin. It was meant for her — her home! He had built it for her. Between long and strenuous hunting trips, he had worked through the winter, felling the trees for logs, and clearing the land so that her dream could come true.

There was no holding back the tears of joy this time, and Emmie let them fall down her cheeks like babbling brooks, and somehow, Luke knew they were tears of joy and gladness, and grabbed her from Ebony's back and swung her around and around. Together, they ran, hand-in-hand, to the crude skin door, and he held it aside for her to enter. Her eyes could not believe what they were seeing. A lovely room, with a loft for sleeping. The cabin was fully stocked and ready for them. Many sizes of baskets hung on pegs on the wall, and there were clay pots and bowls on a crude table. A fire pit had been dug in the very middle of the room, directly beneath an opening in the roof.

Emmie quickly threw off her shawl and began to investigate the contents of the bowls. Dried fish, fruit, berries and smoked meats were there, and in the corner, in a large, hamper-like basket, she found corn meal. She then climbed to the loft and bounced upon the bed of soft boughs, which were covered with a bear skin. Luke quickly followed her, and they lay together for several minutes, looking lovingly into each others eyes. He pulled her to him and began to caress her tenderly. Impulsively, Emmie leaned over him and placed her lips on his and kissed him long and hard. He finally drew from her, and looked puzzeledly at her, and she immediately realized that kissing was a foreign act to him, and so she softly uttered the word "kiss" several times. He smiled, and repeated after her, "kiss," and kissed her hard several times.

Emmie was soon to realize that there was more to marriage than living and working together. One night, after Luke had tenderly made love to her, she lay and wondered at all the things Ma had taught her, about herself and about him. She wondered about Ma and Papa, and if they had made love like she and Luke, and why Ma had not told her about so wonderful an experience. Ma had taught her many things; to cook and sew and knit, and to read and write; to care for animals and tend a garden, and how to make things grow. But Ma had never said one word about love or marriage. She had mentioned many times, while teaching Emmie, all the ways of caring for a home, that Emmie would someday have a home of her own, but never were there any words of love or loving a man the way she now loved Luke.

The young couple started right in, readying their land for planting, and they worked side by side, clearing and cultivating the soil. They spent long, hard hours felling trees and pulling stumps, using their horses as work helpers. Emmie often felt sorry for the horses, especially Ebony, but his lean, strong body only seemed to thrive under all the work, and no matter how tired she was when the sun set, she always took time to rub him down, and pat him in a sort of "thank you" way for his help.

When their crop of corn was planted and had begun to grow, they fenced it all in so that no animals could get at the tiny, succulent sprouts and ruin it. During the summer months Emmie ventured a short distance into the forest and brought back wild plants and bushes and planted them in rows by the front of the cabin. Luke laughed at these little rows of flowers, telling her partly by words and partly by actions, that the woods were full of such flowers, and he often brought some to her from his hunting trips.

Each evening, as they sat by their fire, they taught each other their language, and soon Emmie found herself speaking as much Indian as English, and Luke doing the same thing. He was a very apt student, and he enjoyed these sessions very much. He learned much from this white princess of his, and he loved her the more dearly for her teaching. The ways of the white man, he found very useful in many ways — a lot of hard work, but the results seemed very rewarding. As the last full moon of summer approached, their larder was well supplied for the winter ahead. The snows came early that fall, but Luke and Emmie were ready, and Emmie soon wished for more to do. Luke had made them crude snow shoes of bent hickory branches, laced with narrow strips of rawhide. These they tied to their feet and took long walks in the forest, gathering fresh boughts for their loft, and fallen branches for firewood.

Chapter IX

Luke hunted alone, and was often gone for two or three days at a time. During these long hours alone, Emmie would grow lonesome and melancholy, but the sight of Luke coming over the knoll with an animal over his shoulders would quickly liven her spirits and please her immensely. On one such return he carried a tiny coyote puppy beneath his jacket. He had found it shivering and alone with an injured leg, and had brought it home to her. She immediately adored it, and called it Bob, for besides its broken leg, he had somehow, in a freak accident, lost most of his tail. Emmie suspected a white man's trap, but said nothing to Luke. For the first time in a long while, she wondered about Papa and the boys. Maybe they were closer to the great river than she had at first imagined. But she didn't have time to dwell long on these thoughts as the little coyote was beginning to whimper, and so she set about trying to fix his leg. She straightened it as best she could, and bound it with a flat stick and a leather strap. He seemed content to lay in her lap and was soon fast asleep. Luke soon came in with some fresh goat's milk, and Emmie made a heaping bowl of hot corn mush for supper. The hot corn, covered with the rich milk, warmed them and took the chill from Luke's bones. While Emmie gathered up the bowls and spoons and washed them, he sprawled out in front of the fire, and the little coyote snuggled up against him. They looked so warm and contented that Emmie crept up to the loft alone, and was soon fast asleep too.

The goats had been a new addition to their little farm, and in fact, their first livestock, in addition to the horses. They had been driven down from the compound late in the fall by a younger brother of Luke, who had also been their first and only visitor. He had been sent, Emmie suspected, by the Chief, to see how they were managing, and had been seemingly pleased at their progress. Their storage bins were full of grain, and the shed they had built to shelter the horses was a fine addition to their cabin. Emmie hadn't realized until this visitor came, what a great sacrifice the Chief had made for her. To allow his oldest son, and bravest warrior, to leave the compound and live like a white man. It was not until many years later that she fully realized how foresighted the Chief was. Even then, in this so newly freed country, the old Chief had recognized the white man as the conqueror, and had wanted his son to be a part of the new world, and not a hunted and feared "redskin."

As Emmie lay alone in the loft, she thought of all these things, and thanked her God that she had been found by such a fine person as Luke.

Emmie kept wishing for things that she remembered at home. Things Ma and Papa had had that would, she thought, make her life and Luke's easier. Not that she ever complained about the many hours she spent toiling in the cabin and in the fields, but she also felt she could make better use of some of their meager supplies if she had some of this equipment. She often drew pictures of these things in the dirt floor, as they sat before the fire in the late evenings. Luke always was interested and amazed with her drawings, and often whittled spoons and paddles that she had drawn, with his precious knife. One of the things she most yearned for was some sort of churn to make butter. They had had more milk than they could use from the goat all last season, and now that the goat was going to have kids, they would once again have an abundant supply.

Emmie had made some pot cheese, but even with that, there was still too much for the two of them. Of course Bob was using up some, but she knew that as soon as his leg was completely healed, he would be off and away, back to the forest, and the milk would once again be a problem. She tried beating the milk in a deep bowl, but only succeeded in splashing herself and everything around her, and so she had given up.

    Luke had watched all this in deep silence, and had said nothing to her, but late one afternoon he came in, ready for the evening meal, and laid beside her bowl a strange looking object that he had obviously labored many hours making. It had a long handle, with a heavy, star-like object at the end. As Emmie sat down, the gift immediately caught her eye. She picked it up and examined it very closely. She waved it around and laid it back down and looked questioningly at him. He jumped up and grabbed a twig from the wood pile, and kneeling to the floor, he quickly sketched a crude churn. Emmie understood immediately, and quickly got a bowl and skimmed some cream from the milk bucket and began to work the new tool back and forth between her palms. In a very short time the cream thickened and curdled and then became butter. With the back of a spoon, she spread this over some warm corn bread and handed it to Luke. He hesitated for several seconds before biting into it. The expression on his face was strange to Emmie, and she thought that surely her butter was a failure, but almost immediately his expression changed, and he swept her up in her arms and swung her around the room many times. She poured the whey off into a cup and sipped it slowly, savoring the taste of the buttery milk, and then offered the cup to Luke, who drank it all and held out the cup for more. What a wonderful gift he had made for her, and she, in turn, with his gift, had made him this wonderful food and drink. He dipped his finger in the bowl and licked the butter from it and smiled at Emmie.

"Butter," Emmie repeated several times, and soon he was repeating the word after her. "Buttermilk," she said, as she lifted the cup to her lips, and he smiled and called it "milk-butter."

Like the milk, they soon had other supplies in excess of their needs. The walls of the cabin were lined with furs, and each of them had a hooded jacket that Emmie had made of rabbit fur, trimmed with raccoon. There were also several fox skins and a small bale of mink.

Emmie had often wondered how far they were from the great river, and after Luke had brought Bob home with the broken leg and bobbed tail, she began to form a plan in her mind. She said not a word to Luke, but through the long winter she thought often of her plan. After all, Papa and the boys had taken hides down the river and traded them for things they needed, so why not she and Luke? Luke must not go alone. She had heard of how many of the white traders at the trading posts had cheated the Indians, and so she waited and planned. They could not both go, she decided. Who would look after the goats and cabin? They had never had any callers, except Luke's brother, but surely, if they left their little farm alone, and someone happened by, there would be thievery and destruction. And so, she decided that she and Ebony must make the trip alone. She knew by the flow of the brook, that if she followed it, she would eventually come to the river.

One early spring evening Emmie set about trying to explain to Luke about her planned trip. The explanation was not nearly as hard as she had imagined. She knew enough of his language, and he of hers, so that with little difficulty, she made him understand that she would return and bring with her the tools and supplies they needed. She could tell from his facial expression and nervous manner, that he was desperately afraid that she would not return. But after much persuasion on her part, he finally consented. And so, after much planning and packing, she was ready for the journey. She had decided to wear the clothes that the Indian squaws had made for her wedding, and Luke looked very pleased when she was finally about to start out.

Ebony was so loaded down that there was hardly room for Emmie, but she managed to squeeze on, between the bales of pelts, and so set off down the creek bank. Luke had made a sheaf for his precious knife, and had made her strap it around her waist, just in case she met up with an unfriendly animal, or would in any way need protection. She felt so very sad as she rode off, never looking back, although she could feel Luke's eyes upon her until she rounded the bend, far downstream from the little cabin.

Chapter X

Emmie rode steadily, but not hard, until the sun was very high before she stopped and refreshed herself in the brook and allowed Ebony to rest and drink and graze on the fresh grasses along the bank. The horse seemed to realize that she was frightened as he wandered, never very far from her. They continued on their way, the ladened horse and girl renewed and refreshed after their rest. The sun was rapidly disappearing before Emmie decided that she would have to spend the night by the brook. She had found no good, sheltered caves, and dared not ride much further, lest she be overtaken by the darkness. And should Ebony stumble, or slip into a pit, she would be in terrible straights. She decided against a fire, although she had become very apt at starting a flame by rubbing two dried hardwood branches together.

She took corn bread and dried fish from her basket and ate heartily, after which, she drank from the brook. She felt sorry that she dare not unload Ebony and allow him more rest and comfort, but she rubbed his neck, and gave him a lump or two of maple sugar from her basket, and decided that was the best that she could do for now. She spread her shawl and curled up, and almost immediately was asleep.

When she awoke, the sun was not yet above the horizon, but the sky was bright, and she could tell from this light patch of sky that she had travelled both south and east on her journey thus far. She splashed cool water over her face, and drank generously. She took a biscuit from her basket and swung her body up on Ebony's back, and they were off. The morning air was cool and felt sharp against her face and hands as she held the reins tightly in her grip. The only life they had seen thus far were a few small animals. The sun soon warmed her, and they travelled steadily, covering, what Emmie thought, must be many miles. Just before noon they came to a small waterfall, and a place where the main stream was joined by a smaller one. Emmie's hopes rose in anticipation of soon finding the river, but it was once again growing dark before she gave up, and ate her evening meal and went to sleep. She was beginning to ache all over. She had never ridden so far before, and she was now in doubt of ever being able to find the river.

As the third day dawned, she was ready to forge on, but had made up her mind that if she didn't come to the river on this day, she would retrace her trail and return to Luke, defeated. But her hopes were to be realized, for just before noon, when her spirits were at their lowest, the brook suddenly widened, and the shores became marshy. She had to slow Ebony's gait considerably, and they picked their way along. She finally slid from his back, and together they worked their way carefully to the river's edge. Almost immediately she saw what she thought was a trail along the opposite bank, but not daring to have Ebony try to swim with his heavy load, they slowly made their way eastward, downstream. By mid-afternoon she could see a cabin ahead on their side of the river, and she swung herself up on Ebony's back and touched his rump lightly and they trotted off toward the house. As she pulled up the reins tight and stopped, she heard voices shouting from the far side of the cabin, and wept with joy as a young woman appeared around the corner, followed by a small child and a dog. The dog started howling, and Ebony drew up short, but Emmie kept her balance, and gently patted him until he was once again calm. The woman, Emmie could now see, was hardly older than herself, and she struggled to hold the hand of the child on one side, and calm the dog on the other. These deeds, both accomplished, she spoke to Emmie, asking a rash of questions. Who was she? Was she alone? Where was she going?

Emmie smiled and answered the questions in order. She was Emmie, wife of Luke. Yes, she was alone, and she would like directions to the nearest trading post. Without hesitation, the woman offered her hand, and helped Emmie down from Ebony's back. Her name was Maria Swenson, she said, and this was her son, Jon. The boy giggled and scuffed the loose soil with his bare feet. They walked together toward the house, and it was not until they were at the door that Emmie realized she still held Ebony's reins, and that he was beside her. She tethered him at the hitching post, and left him to graze as they entered the cool kitchen.

Maria dipped up big mugs of cool milk, and set out a plate of sugar cookies, the first cookies Emmie had seen since the great fire. She ate ravishingly, at last setting down her empty mug. They talked for hours. Emmie doing most of the talking, relating to Maria all the details of her life since she had escaped from the fire. Emmie also impressed her with her now happy life with Luke and her love for him. When she finished, she sat weak and trembling and spent from her reliving all the emotional stress of her unusual tale. Maria stood and put her arm around Emmie's shoulders and they were quiet for several minutes. When Maria felt the trembling subside, she returned to her chair and sat for several more minutes. Finally, she told Emmie that she would like her to spend the night with her; that her husband, George, was down the river at the trading post, and would not be back for at least another day. Emmie agreed and went out to see to Ebony and her cargo. Maria and the boy joined her, and together they unloaded Ebony and dragged the bales inside. Maria was amazed at the fine quality of the pelts, and assured Emmie that they would no doubt bring a high price. As soon as they had taken care of the cargo and the horse, they turned their attention to Maria's chores, and with them accomplished, they returned to the house and supper.

They lingered over the meal until Jon nearly toppled from his stool, having fallen asleep at his place. Maria gathered him in her arms and tenderly laid him in a small bunk, built in the wall, beside the fireplace. The two women did up the few dishes and sat by the fire and visited long into the night. They figured out from Emmie's description of her father's homestead, that at the time of the fire, when she had crossed the river in her confusion, Emmie had run northwesterly, and had covered many more miles than would have been possible for her under normal conditions, and had actually been relatively close to Canada when Luke found her. But Maria reassured her that she thought with the quailty of the cargo, they would do very well, and her long trip would not be in vain.

Emmie rested well, and when she awoke the next morning, she found that Maria and Jon had already eaten and had gone to do the morning chores. Maria had set out a basin for her, and she washed slowly, using warm water from the great iron kettle at the fireplace. She had finished and was dressed when they returned with milk and eggs. Maria fixed her a hearty breakfast of pork and eggs and hot biscuits, and Emmie ate with relish. Then the two women, under little Jon's watchful eye, loaded the cargo back onto Ebony, and Emmie was ready to continue her journey. She promised to stop on her return trip, and both women were sad at the parting.

It was only a short day's ride to the post, and with such a fine early start, Emmie was confident that she and Ebony would make it in good time. The sun was just slipping toward the west when the trail widened and Emmie could detect smoke rising and sounds ahead. As she approached the small settlement, she noted many Indians sitting around with small kegs of rum, and was now doubly certain that her decision to come alone was for the best. She rode more slowly as she approached the post, and many thoughts flashed through her mind. Where would she sleep, here among all these men? So far, she had not seen a single woman. And how would she make out, a woman bartering with the gruff men? But her safety, and Ebony's were foremost in her mind. She rode directly to the main building, and slipping off Ebony's back, she tied him to the rail, patting him reassuringly. She turned and strode, as if with great confidence, into the post. No one was more surprised than Emmie to find the trader a small, balding, elderly man, with spectacles. Emmie was so taken back that she could hardly speak. For some reason, she had expected a big, burly rough and ready person, with a beard, and perhaps, even slightly unkempt. But she quickly recovered and told him of her cargo, and without even speaking to her he went out with her to inspect it. His expression never changed, but he whistled a shrill note, and an old man, rather bent over, and with large gnarled hands, appeared and together they unloaded the furs and took them inside. As the trader untied each bale, his eyes showed great delight. When he opened and inspected the last one, he paused and then asked Emmie why she was dressed as an Indian princess, which she surely was not. The long blond hair, blue eyes and fair skin were not the features of any Indian he had ever known. She hesitated, wondering what his reaction would be if she told him her story, and this hesitation saved her temporarily, at least, from having to say anything.

He turned and stepped to the rear of the room, and pushing a door open, called to someone to come. As he spoke, Emmie noted that his voice went with neither his stature or face. He had a deep, booming voice, very commanding, and although he had questioned her gently, his command call now could not be mistaken. A rather stout lady, in the most exotic dress that Emmie had ever seen, appeared in the doorway. She stood head and shoulders above the trader, but Emmie could tell by her expression that she obeyed his every command.

"Yes, Mr. Becker?" she asked meekly. This was Emmie's first clue as to the trader's name. He brusquely told her that this girl was supposedly alone, and would no doubt need lodging for the night. She nodded and smiled, and as she spoke, Emmie thought, "What beautiful teeth and complexion the woman had." Her face looked all creamy and rosy, and her teeth were pearly white, but her smile was so sad-like that Emmie wondered how she had come to live in this far away place with this little old man. She was soon to find the woman's story nearly as bizarre as her own. She asked Emmie's name, and held out her hand to her and welcomed her to her home. Mr. Becker intervened, telling his wife that they would join her when they had completed their business. Some time later, after he had been counting skins and examining them for some time, he whistled again and the little man reappeared. Mr. Becker directed him to lock up for the night, and to care for the princess's horse. This was the first time, since questioning her, that he had referred to her as a princess, and Emmie was truly amazed. It was also at this point that she realized that she had not answered his questions. In fact, she had not uttered even one word. Perhaps he thought she knew very little English, just enough to tell him of her cargo. She must set this straight immediately. She started to relate her tale to him, and surprisingly, he listened intently. But when she had finished, he simply told her to go into Mrs. Becker, and she would provide her with the necessities to freshen, and that he would join them shortly.

The living rooms Emmie found were amazing. She had never seen such furniture in her life. She could not even imagine that such things existed. The most amazing thing of all to Emmie was a mirror that hung on the wall. Emmie had never seen herself in a mirror. She had seen her reflection in the clear, still pools at the coves in the stream, and had often gazed for hours at hers and other reflections in the spring at Papa's farm when she was a little girl. But seeing an image of her whole self reflected from the glass on the wall both amazed and frightened her, and she began to sob. Mrs. Becker put her plump arm around her shoulders and comforted her. She quickly recovered and proceded to wash and straighten her hair and smooth her dress as best she could, and soon realized how hungry she was. She had been so intent on reaching the post before sundown that she hadn't even stopped for lunch. Just long enough for Ebony to have a long, cool drink, and they had continued right on.

The meal was a hearty one, although not as hearty as Emmie was accustomed to. There were foods that Emmie had never tasted before, and the sharp spices puckered her unaccustomed lips and tongue, and she drank several cups of hot tea to ease the smarting. After supper, Mr. Becker returned to the store and left Mrs. Becker and Emmie alone to visit. A small Indian girl came in and cleared away the food and dishes, and Emmie felt that the girl's eyes were upon her every moment. Now that Emmie had seen her full reflection in the wall mirror, she realized how unlike the Indians she looked, and how puzzling a picture she must present to them.

Chapter XI

Mrs. Becker told her story first. She had been born of a relatively wealthy family south of Albany, and had known no hardships in her younger life. She had married, as a young lady, a handsome, dashing officer in General Washington's Army, and after the war he had persuaded her to travel west with him. He had heard from the Indians about the great salt mines beyond the fork of the great river, and knowing the value of this mineral, he wanted to settle near the mines and work them. And so, they had gathered together their belongings, with the furniture that her father had given them as a wedding gift, and had spent all their money on wagons and tools, and had set out for the west. The going had been slow and hard, and after they had passed Fort Schuyler, just beyond Fort Dayton, they had found the wagons almost impossible to maneuver. There were only narrow paths, and these, they found, sometimes wandering almost twice the distance necessary. But they were young, and believing that their future and fortune lay ahead, they had somehow forged on ahead.

It had been four days since they had seen a white man, and for the first time she began to doubt that they could go on much farther. They camped for the night in the open, as they had travelled south, away from the river to avoid the swamplands, and it was in this clearing that they had been attacked by a small, lone, stray band of Red-coats and Indians. All but one of their wagons had been destroyed, and she and Mr. Becker, their wagon-master, had been the only survivors. When the sun rose the following morning, their camp lay in utter ruin. Her bridegroom lay near her wagon, dead, and the rest of the party — every one of them dead from the tomahawks and guns of the raiders.

She and Mr. Becker had worked for two days, burying the dead, and then another day was spent in trying to round up the horses. They had been able to find and rope two, and even so, she had wanted to continue on. And so just she and Mr. Becker had forged on, westward. When they had travelled on for several days (but covering only a few miles), and they were exhausted, they camped. Mr. Becker suggested that they stay and rest for a few days and reassemble their thoughts, and while they camped, she had been taken by some sort of fever and had been ill for several weeks. When she was well enough to travel, they retraced their steps to where the creek turned east and joined the lake outlet and became the great river.

They had decided to set up a trading post with the supplies that they had been able to salvage from the raid. This post, where she now rested, was the result of all that. They had been here for many years now, and from their meager start, had grown to be very prosperous. That first year they had worked from their wagon, to which Mr. Becker added a lean-to. During the next summer he built them their first cabin. They had help from some friendly Indians that worked endlessly for a jug of rum and some trinkets.

As more and more people moved westward, they had expanded their post until it was as Emmie found it today. In the second year she had wed Mr. Becker, and had had a good life — not what she had planned when she had started out those many years ago, but she had been well cared for and happy. And the descendants of some of the very Indians that had killed her young husband and had brought her young dreams to an end were now her friends and servants.

It was Emmie's turn to tell her story, but she was at last feeling exhaustion from her trip, and she wondered to herself where she was going to sleep. Mrs. Becker recognized her condition and summoned the Indian girl, who led Emmie to a room at the left of the main room, a bedroom. To be sure, it was a very tiny room, but it held a real bed — something that Emmie had never slept in, not even at home with Ma and Papa. They had a bed, but she and the boys had had mats, filled with soft straw, on the floor of the loft. As Emmie turned around, there, right beside her, was a small chest with a bowl and a pitcher on the top, and hanging on the wall, another mirror. This one not as large as the one in the main room, but large enough, nevertheless, to reflect her image from her waist to the top of her head. Emmie looked at her reflection, and as she did, the candle flames flickerings made strange shadows dance all around her, and with this picture of herself still dancing in her head, she blew out the candle and lay down on the bed. She pulled the quilt up over her, and was immediately asleep.

It was well past daybreak before she opened her eyes again. The unaccustomed surroundings puzzled her for a few moments, and she thought she must be dreaming, but was brought back quickly to reality with a soft rap at the door. It was the Indian girl with warm water, and so she arose and washed and joined Mrs. Becker in the main room. She was very hungry, and this time the food was more familiar to her tastes. Pork and eggs and biscuits, with butter and honey, and strong, black coffee. Emmie ate and ate, with the astonished Mrs. Becker watching carefully. Where did that girl put all that food, and still keep her body so thin and beautiful? Mrs. Becker wished for her secret.

Emmie had a list in her mind of the things that she would like to take back with her to the little farm. Tools for Luke, and all sorts of utensils for the cabin and also a few chickens were included in this list. She had been dreaming about these things for two years, and the list grew regularly until now she realized that she would have to decide on just a few of the most essential items. Mr. Becker appeared almost as soon as she had finished breakfast, and explained that if she were ready, they should go into the store and settle their business. Emmie was ready.

Without ado, Mr. Becker opened the drawer under the counter and took out a huge ledger, which he opened, and began to read from it to Emmie. She was both shocked and delighted. What he was reading was an account of the skins and furs she had brought to him, and what prices he would pay. He had separated them into lots. A term that Emmie was not familiar with, but which she comprehended to mean the bales or bundles of the different kinds of furs, et cetera. The total figure he quoted to Emmie was, in her mind, astronomical. Far above her wildest dreams, and, in fact, she could not imagine that much money. She was so stunned she could neither shout or weep for joy, but just stood, as if in a trance. She was brought back to reality with the booming of the little man's voice as he asked her for her list, so that he might get her things ready for her. Her list, of course, was in her mind, and she didn't know where to start. She could have all the things she had dreamed of, and even more. And so she started to babble away to Mr. Becker.

"Slow down, girl," he said, as he drew out a paper and pen and began to write. Emmie had never seen anyone write on paper with a pen. She had had a slate as a young child, but even Ma had not had paper and pen, and so she must have some of each of these. Mr. Becker advised her against the pen, and showed her instead some sticks of charcoal, used to write with, and so a small box of these were set aside for her.

   The practical side of Emmie surfaced immediately, and she asked that a slate and slate pencils also be added to her list. Her list nearly completed, she walked around the post and looked at all the things yet to choose from. She selected a small Bible for herself, and a dress-length of blue material, and a small pair of crude scissors, luxuries she hadn't even been able to dream about. For Luke, she chose a knife in a fancy sheath, and an axe. She passed over the guns. Guns frightened her, and they would need ammunition and supplies which she felt were unnecessary. Luke had been brought up to use the bow and arrow, and so she would leave it at that. Six chickens were the last luxury item that she chose. Mr. Becker told her that she could go back and visit with his wife if she chose, and he would take care of getting her things together. But she first asked about Ebony, and hurried around behind the post to the shed where he was being kept.

   He had never been confined in his life, and was quite jittery, but calmed down at the sight of Emmie. She patted and brushed him and took a lump of maple sugar from her saddle bag for him. After this, she retraced her steps and found Mrs. Becker in the living room, waiting for her. She told Emmie that Mr. Becker had related Emmie's story to her last night, and was she sure she wanted to go back and live in the mountains with the Indians? Emmie was astounded. No such thought had ever entered her head, and she quickly told Mrs. Becker that, and she also reaffirmed her love for Luke, and lastly that she now knew no other way of life. He had saved her life, and had given up his way of living for hers, and so she must return as soon as was possible, and she quickly started to gather up her possessions.

"Slow down, girl," Mrs. Becker said, rather sharply. "I meant no harm, only that a girl so beautiful and young as you seemed wasted in the mountains."

But Emmie did not agree, and continued her preparations for leaving. Mr. Becker came in, and speaking directly to Emmie, told her two astonishing facts. She had spent less than half of her credit, and the things that she had chosen could not possibly be all loaded on her horse. What did she want to do? Seeing the astonished look come over Emmie's face, he offered a suggestion. He had a mule he could sell her. She could use this animal as a pack animal, and that would solve more than half of her problems. The rest of the credit she could take in the form of a credit slip, and he would hold it for her return another time. This seemed agreeable to Emmie. When he opened his account book to enter Emmie's credits, he asked for her full name, and without hesitation, she replied, "Emmaline Van der Veer."

Mr. Becker's expression revealed amazement, and Emmie hastened to explain that she had given her maiden name. She was, as she had previously told him, married to an Indian, and since Luke, although not an outcast, was no longer considered a tribal member, and since she felt he would need more than Luke and Emmie for his records, she was sure her Papa would approve of them using his name. And so the account was set up in the name of Luke and

Emmaline Van der Veer, and then the packing began. She must spend another night at the post in order to get an early start, as with two animals, the trip would be slowed considerably.

And so, as the sun rose on a bright, clear day, Emmie and Ebony were ready. The mule was a small animal, but Mr. Becker assured her that he was well-behaved, and they were all finally ready to start. Mrs. Becker hugged and kissed her, and bade her to return soon, and made it most clear that she would always be welcome. She called her the "Adirondack Princess."

Emmie was astride Ebony and ready to leave, when George Swenson came from downstream, where he had gone to visit relatives. When he learned where Emmie was headed, and that she had spent a night at his home with his wife on her down-trip, he asked her to wait a bit until he gathered his waiting supplies and rode off with her. Emmie was glad for the company. Even though she was anxious to return to Luke, she had not anticipated the lonely trip. They made excellent time as George knew the trail well, and was most anxious about Maria and Jon. He had not expected to be away so long, but when he had reached the post he had received word of his brother's illness, and so had journeyed on to visit with him. He was glad that he had. It was good to see his brother again after so many years, but the illness had turned out to be not very serious, and now George was anxious to return home and get started with his spring planting.

They reached the Swenson farm in good time, and Maria and Jon, who had been concerned over George's tardiness, came to meet them. They were glad too, to see Emmie, and Maria wanted to hear what was in all the bundles. She laughed at the basket of chickens, and wished Emmie well on her trip up the stream. Emmie continued on until darkness fell. She wanted to get over the swampland and upstream as far as possible. She was sad at leaving all her new friends, but was excited and anxious to see Luke and show him all the things she had for them. She didn't bother with a fire, or even boughs to sleep on, but spread her cape under a tall pine and slept well. She woke before the sun was up, and after watering the animals, she jumped on Ebony, and they were again on their way. Although the trip back was at times up hill, she seemed to be able to travel faster than when she had started out. Ebony had only herself and saddlebags to carry, and the little mule fared well beneath his load. The chickens kept up a continual squawking, and the second day, when she stopped at noon to rest, she made a terrible mistake. She let them loose, thinking they needed exercise, and perhaps more water than they were getting from the bowls she had been offering them. They immediately scattered, and instead of resting, she spent a great deal of time, much longer than she had planned for the stop, getting them back together. When the chickens were finally all rounded up, and back in the basket, Emmie was exhausted, hot and dirty. She stepped into the brook and let the cool water run over her body for several minutes. She splashed her face and hair and stepped up on the bank, and shook herself as an animal might, and stripping a piece of willow bark with Luke's knife, she tied back her hair and was ready to continue on.

Ebony was well rested, and the mule also, and so

they stepped along lively and were well toward the cabin before the sun began to set. Emmie thought better of going on in the dusk, and so made camp. For the first time, on either trip, she built a fire and dried her damp clothes. She sat by her fire for a long time and tried to imagine the look on Luke's face when she arrived with all the supplies and the mule, besides. She fell asleep musing about a name for the animal, but none that she felt suitable came to mind.

Her morning trip was even shorter than she had thought, for before the sun was even halfway to noon, she spotted the cabin through the pines. At first she didn't see Luke working at plowing the cornfield. He spotted her first and dropped the plow and came running to meet her. Out of breath as he was, he swung her from Ebony's back and held her close and kissed her long and hard. He was so very glad to have her back. Together they led the animals through the gate and right to the door of the cabin. Emmie introduced the little animal to Luke as "Mule," and that was the name that he answered to for the rest of his life.

Luke could not wait to see what was in the bundles, but Emmie had to run in and see her little house. He had kept it spotless, and she thought to herself he had learned the white man's ways well. There was a low fire in the pit, and a large pot of stew was simmering over it; more than they could possibly eat in days, but Emmie was glad that he had prepared for her homecoming, and told him in both her language and his, how happy she was.

Going back outside, they unloaded Mule and brought the bundles inside, Luke treating each one very gently. He was puzzled at the basket of chickens, and Emmie cautioned him not to let them loose, explaining that they would have to make a fenced-in place for them to keep them safe from other animals, and to keep them from straying away. She would tell him about her experiences with them at a later time. The mule, she explained, would help with the plowing and logging, and that by using him, the horses would not have to work so hard. Luke seemed more amazed as each package was opened, exclaiming and jumping around like a child. Some, and in fact, most of the things he had never seen before. They stopped and ate some of his stew before Emmie handed him the last package, the one that contained the axe and the knife. When he saw the axe, his eyes shone, and for the first time since she had known him, great tears welled up in his eyes and rolled down his cheeks. Without stopping to say a word to her, he ran outside and across the clearing to the edge of the forest and felled a huge tree. He stood with his foot on the log and the axe held high over his head, and smiled at Emmie.

When they sat by their fire that evening, he kept both the axe and the knife by his side, and when they climbed into their little loft, he took them with him, and slid them under the fresh boughs that he had placed there while she had been gone. When Emmie awoke, she heard the thud of the axe and knew that Luke had already started to fell more trees and clear more land. She hurried and dressed and ran outside to see if he had eaten, but he was on the other side of the pines, deep in the woods, and so she set about her morning chores. She got water and fresh hay for the horses, and she cracked some corn for the chickens. As she ate, she decided the most important chore would be to build some sort of enclosure for the chickens, and so, with Luke's old knife, she went to the brook and gathered branches from the overhanging willow trees. She made several trips to the brook from the cabin before she started the actual pen. She wove flat, mat-like sides, and as her fingers flew, weaving the fine, supple branches together, her mind rushed back, to think of all the things she had brought, and how much easier their life would be. In the distance she could hear the ring of the axe as Luke chopped into tree after tree.

Her work went well, and the time passed quickly, and stopping only for a cup of tea and a biscuit, she had finished long before Luke came home for supper. With the chickens all secure in their new pen, Emmie watered the animals and milked the goat, and when Luke returned, she was writing on the slate. Her letters amused him, and he wondered why she thought the slate was so important. Drawing in the dirt had seemed so natural to him.

Emmie had a great plan in her mind. She would teach Luke all that she knew. Ma had taught her a great deal. Ever since she had been about five years old, Emmie had been taught at home by Ma. There was no school that she could go to, but Ma had a big thought about learning, and had made Emmie and the boys study some each day. As the boys grew older and big enough to help Papa in the fields, Ma had been able to spend more time with Emmie. Papa would sometimes make remarks about too much learning would make a person "funny." But he always patted

Emmie and praised her when she did well, and now she was about to embark on a teaching career of her own.

Luke had taught her many things, and now she wanted to repay him with what she knew. She had already taught him how to communicate, through pictures, anything he couldn't make her understand any other way. And so, after their evening meal had been cleared away, they sat outside the door in the cool spring evening air, and the first lesson began. Luke proved to be even more apt than Emmie had even anticipated, and had soon progressed from just writing numbers, to doing sums. And when she felt he was ready, and could comprehend the greatness of it, she told him of all the credit they had at Mr. Becker's post. She told how his furs and skins were far superior to any others; that she had been paid the top price. Mr. Becker, at her request, had given Emmie one small gold coin, and this she now showed to him. His eyes shone with excitement, and he was more eager than ever to learn the ways of the white man. But Emmie cautioned him that many of his ways were superior, and that he must never give in to an easier way; that in the long run, together, they would have to combine their knowledge and ways, and hopefully, they would choose the best of both; and if they were cautious and did this, they would be able to succeed beyond either of their wildest dreams.

Emmie had only been back about a week when she discovered the first hen's egg. She was so excited and made such a fuss that Luke could hardly understand what had happened. An egg was not, he thought, anything to get so excited about. In the spring the woods were full of nests with eggs in them, but after several mornings of finding an egg or two, he began to see that Emmie's hens might be an asset after all. She wove a special basket for her eggs to hang high, near the roof of the cabin, and before long they had more than they could use.

When they had the ground worked up and their cornfield planted, Luke started on another room for their cabin. Emmie had drawn him a picture of what she wanted, and with his new axe to work with, he forged ahead excitedly. Emmie had found a pit of clay near the west side of the brook, and she spent many long hours making brick-shaped objects, and drying them in the sun. With Ebony's help, and using Mule too, she dragged large slabs of slate up from the bed of the brook, and before long she had enough supplies to build a small fireplace on one side of the new addition. The lean-to would have to be enlarged also before fall, she explained to Luke, because Mule would also need to be sheltered from the winter weather. The shed, as it was, was barely big enough for their horses. And what about her precious hens? Winter quarters, which also would be necessary for them, would have to be made. All these plans and the work involved, never seemed to dampen their enthusiasm, and the days passed quickly. By midsummer, all their projects were well on their way to completion.

Chapter XII

It was very early — before dawn — when they were aroused by a commotion in the yard. Luke quickly darted out, with Emmie right behind him, to find two young braves from Luke's tribe arriving. They seemed exhausted, and apparently had ridden through the darkness to arrive at such an early hour. They quickly related their message. Luke's father was ill and apparently dying, and had requested to see his son and the Princess. So they had been dispatched to bring them back. Many thoughts flew through

Emmie's mind. She had not seen any of the tribe except Luke's younger brother, who had visited them during their first summer, and she was saddened to think that their visit would be shrouded by death, and would they be asked to give up all they had worked for, to return and have Luke as their leader? She had wanted to visit the compound for several weeks now, but they had been so very busy with the new room and the fireplace, and the shed, that she had not suggested a visit to Luke.

She quickly gathered a few things together, and while she was making herself ready, Luke instructed the two braves, who would stay there while they were away, to tend the livestock, and what had to be done. She heard him emphasize the necessity of gathering the eggs so that they did not attract any weasels or mink, and about watering the mule and goats. Most of the animals at the compound were allowed to roam free, but these on their little farm were kept fenced in, and must be tended. The braves thought this very foolish, "mostly women's work," they muttered, but promised to do their best. They were fascinated by Luke's axe, but he did not leave it behind, instead, he tied it to his knapsack, and they were soon ready. Their horses were fresh and so they made good time and they reached the village by sundown. Luke was taken directly to his father, and was gone, what seemed to Emmie, a very long time. She had imagined returning for a visit, and how she would tell all the squaws about the trading post, and would be showing off her new dress, but the camp was very solemn, and Emmie quickly decided that all her news could keep, and she, of course, had not had time to hardly think of the new material or the dress she hoped to make. When Luke came out from the Chief's tepee, everyone had gathered around the central fire, which was now very low. As he came out, the old squaw who had tended Emmie those many moons ago, rose and went inside, closing the flap behind her.

Luke came directly to Emmie and told her of the very weak condition of his father, but even so, he wanted to hold a council meeting, and so he would arrange it. He would not wait for morning for it might be too late then, but immediately started quietly giving orders. Everyone quickly heeded his instructions and were soon ready for the meeting. The fire was soon blazing high and the flames seemed to dance in the sky. The women all retired to the main tepee that was used only in bad, rainy weather, and sat quietly. Most of the children slept, and the few that didn't, seemed to sense the gravity of the situation, and were very still. They could hear from their retreat the commotion as the old, sick Chief was assisted outside to conduct the meeting. His voice was weak and trembling, and the women could not understand what he was saying. The meeting, to Emmie, seemed to go on for some time, and her anxiety mounted as she felt her future with Luke depended on what the old Chief was saying. There seemed to be a long lull. A young brave appeared at the flap of the tepee and bade her to come with him. He took her to the Chief, and as everyone sat silently and listened to the old man — weak and tremendously exhausted from the ordeal — talked to Emmie. He talked for several minutes, relating to Emmie in his native tongue what he had decided. He was about to enter a new life, he told her, but before he left on his journey, he must name someone to lead his people. His oldest son would naturally be his choice, but his son loved her and he respected that. He told her that he felt Luke had learned well the things that Emmie had taught him, and his ways were now the ways of the white man, and although he could command that he return, he would not, and so he would name Luke's brother to be the chief of the tribe. He too loved Emmie and bade her to come close so he could feel her soft white skin, and feel her silken, golden hair. As he held her and repeated "Mountain Princess" several times, he slumped over, and was quickly carried into his tepee by the braves. She rose and returned to the other women, and they all sat quietly through the night.

When daybreak came, Luke came and told her that his father had died, and they must all make ready for his burial, and to welcome his brother as their new leader.

The ceremony over, and order reigning once more in the village with the new Chief in command, Emmie and Luke made preparations to leave for their home. They had been away longer than Emmie had expected, and she now worried about their animals and garden, and there was much work to do on their building before harvest time. With their horses and themselves ready, a new situation arose.

A young maiden begged to go with them. She could be of great help to them, and could be company for Emmie when Luke was off hunting and trapping when the snows came. And so, without very much ado, it was decided to take the girl with them. Emmie could use the help, and she would surely enjoy the companionship when she would be alone for many days at a time during the long winter months. The girl was given a young pony, and since she had few possessions, it took her a very short time to ready herself for the journey.

The trip back down the mountain went well, and although the sun had nearly disappeared in the west before they came in sight of the cabin, they had covered the miles swiftly. Emmie was the first one to jump down and run to the chicken pen to see her precious hens. The braves were glad to see them, and welcomed them heartily, and pressed them for news of events at the village. They all went inside, and as Emmie prepared an evening meal, Luke related all that had happened. The braves were saddened at the death of their old Chief, but seemed pleased for Luke; that as the old man's last act, he had excused him from leadership, and had made his brother the new Chief.

With the dawn they were all up, and the braves were off, back to their camp and families, and Emmie and Luke set about resuming their chores and building. They found all their animals had been well tended, but were nearly overcome with the quantity of eggs and milk that had accumulated during their absence. The young maiden's Indian name, translated to "Spring Flower" in English, and it was Emmie's decision to call her "Violet," the loveliest, Emmie thought, of all the spring flowers. With this decided, she set about showing Violet how to skim the cream from the bowls of milk, and to make butter. Leaving the girl to tend to this, she joined Luke, and they were quickly engrossed in cultivating their corn. The crop was hearty and healthy and promised to be bountiful, and the summer months flew by. Their building progressed well, and the new room was soon ready. Emmie's plans for the room were changed with the addition of Violet to their family, and so she decided that a corner near the new fireplace should be screened off, and Violet could use this for her sleeping quarters. Violet was pleased at these arrangements, as she had never known any private quarters back at the compound. She had shared the family tepee with her brother and sisters, and this private corner was like a palace to her.

With all their projects under control, and not being so exhausted as to literally fall into their beds directly after their evening meal, Emmie and Luke resumed their lessons. Emmie read each evening from her Bible, and he worked on his letters and sums. Violet's interest in their evening's activities was so keen that they soon included her, and Emmie found she had a new very apt student.

After the harvest had been completed and everything secured for the long winter, Luke readied his traps, his bow and arrows, and sharpened his knife in preparation for trips into the forest for fresh meat, furs and skins. Emmie had not had time to think about her bright material she had bought in the spring from Mr. Becker until after Luke had left on his first trip of the season. When she took out the package and spread out the bright cloth, she found Mr. Becker had included a spool of thread and two steel needles. She was delighted, but when she saw the look on Violet's face, as she saw the material spread out, she quickly decided that she could wait for her dress, and would make the material into a dress for Violet. The girl was delighted, and they worked on the garment, creating as they went, and by the time that Luke returned, they had the dress nearly completed.

Luke had not had a very successful trip, but the winter had just begun, and their supply of fresh meat was holding well. After resting a few days, he started out again, and Emmie was happy that Violet was with her, as a great storm swept down upon them, and the howling winds and drifting snow made the days and nights as if one, and she surely would have been more worried and very lonesome without her. Their daily chores took double the normal time as the cold and snow slowed them considerably. They were exhausted from their work, and from worry about the animals. Their supply of firewood was more than ample, and they kept the fire high at all times. The horses and mule and the goats were huddled together, their shed providing sufficient shelter, and they fared well, but Emmie worried about her chickens, and finally decided to move them inside. She and Violet cornered off a place in the original room by piling firewood high and placing a basket of hay in one corner. It was a very crude enclosure, but the hens didn't seem to mind, and they all thrived very well.

Luke's second trip was more successful, but he was exhausted when he finally made his way back to the cabin. He had fashioned a litter-like affair, and had dragged his heavy load for many miles through the cold and high snow drifts. He was utterly spent. Emmie and Violet helped him inside and fixed him a bough mat in front of the new fireplace, and he lay there, resting for some time while Emmie and Violet unloaded the litter and brought the meat and skins inside. He was soon warm and dry, and glad to be back home for a few days. Emmie's thick venison gravy and biscuits were a welcome change for him from the dried cold foods he had survived on these past weeks. Emmie urged him to give up hunting until the storms subsided, but he insisted that his traps must be tended, and so he started out the next morning, with a promise to not go too deep into the forested hills, and to return sooner than before. He kept his promise, and returned as soon as he had gathered the catch from his trap lines. The weather was really growing wild indeed, and he gathered his traps as he unloaded each one, and returned to the cabin with a full bounty, but also with the traps. That meant that unless the weather broke, and he could return soon and reset his line, that the cargo to the post would be very meager. They knew that the animals had to be taken in the late fall and early winter, when their coats were at their maximum thickness, and the carcasses had to be skinned and the hides cured as soon as possible for maximum strength and durability. Unless the weather broke soon none of this would be possible. He paced about the cabin until Emmie thought he might burst from despair, but there was no break in the weather, and snow and cold seemed to sift into the cabin through the most minute cracks.

When not pacing and going outside to check the weather, Luke chopped firewood with his precious axe. Their supply was ample to begin with, and now there were stacks of logs everywhere. The wood ashes and the manure from the horse shed Emmie was piling together at the edge of the cornfield, and explained to Luke and Violet that these she would spread over the land, and that the land would be more fertile, and because of it, their corn would grow taller and stronger, and perhaps their harvest could be doubled without enlarging the area of the plot. This all seemed very strange and thoroughly foreign to both of them, but Emmie's piles continued to grow, and no one interfered with her plans.

Chapter XIII

Spring was late that year, and when the weather broke, Emmie started to ready herself for her trip to the post. Violet agreed to stay at the farm and take care of the necessary chores and this time Luke would accompany her on the trip.

She had never seen him so excited. Of course they would not realize nearly so much as last year from their furs and hides. With the bad weather, the take had been much smaller than usual, and besides, last year there had been an accumulation of two seasons, and Emmie prayed that Luke would not be too disappointed. They rode off at sunup the first morning in May. Emmie on Ebony, and Luke on his pony, and the mule following close on a short rein. The great quantity of melting snow had forced the little brook over its banks in many places, and the travel was slow, and at times very hard. When they reached the flat lands, there were floods, and they had to retrace their steps and detour around what had been merely boggy swamps the spring before. In doing this, they came to the great river east of the Swenson farm, and this was a great disappointment to Emmie. She had wanted to see and visit with Maria and show off Luke to her friend. When they finally arrived at the post, they had been on the trail even longer than it had taken Emmie the year before, and they were very tired and hungry.

Mr. Becker welcomed Emmie warmly and shook hands heartily with Luke. He called to Mrs. Becker, and she appeared immediately. Her warm smile and friendly welcome won Luke over at once, and he and Emmie followed her through the post and into her living quarters. Luke was very obviously taken back, as he did not even imagine that places like this existed. Even in his wildest dreams he had never conjured up such furnishing as met his eyes. He had learned much from Emmie, but could instantly see that there was much more he must learn of the white man's most unusual ways. He stood motionless, surveying the room, when suddenly his eyes came to the mirror. Emmie thought his eyes would pop from their sockets. He slowly walked toward the wall, and put his hand on the mirror and realized that the image he saw was his own. He turned and swung Emmie around and around. When he finally put her down, her head was reeling, but she was smiling, and so was he. He excitedly asked if they could buy the mirror, but Emmie quickly explained that nothing in the house was for sale, just in the store. The disappointment showed greatly on his face, so she quickly went on to say that perhaps some day Mr. Becker could order a mirror from the city at the mouth of the great river, for them, but now they needed more tools and seeds and necessary supplies. And so, reluctantly, he accepted Emmie's decisions.

Luke had never sat in a chair at a table, and eaten food with anything but his fingers, or a crude wooden spoon, and he was very uncomfortable during the evening meal. He did not understand being waited on by the young Indian girl who lived with the Beckers as their servant. The ways of these white people were even more strange to him than the ways he had learned from Emmie. Until he had found Emmie alone and hurt, he had thought all women were the same, and were to work and tend to their men. But Emmie had been so different. A true Princess, he thought, and so he had tried hard to learn her ways. When they had been married and had left the compound to live alone, Emmie had worked beside him, but now, here she was being tended to as if perhaps she was ill, and he knew she was not. He watched Emmie closely, and tried hard to do as she did, and he managed surprisingly well.

Emmie rearranged her list of purchases in her mind, and put plates and knives and forks at the very top. After the meal was over Mr. Becker and Luke went outside to see to the cargo they had brought with them, and turned the animals over to the old hunchback to be fed and bedded down for the night. Luke had an opportunity to look around the post while Mr. Becker was putting away some ledgers and securing things for the night. He returned to Emmie with many questions. They retired to the little bedroom and talked long into the night.

Everything in the room was foreign to him. The bed, high off the floor; the quilts instead of fur robes or skins; the pillows, soft and filled with the down of geese; the stand that held the wash bowl and pitcher; and the chamber pot in the compartment below; cloth to wet and wash your body with; and more and larger pieces of cloth to dry away the water. All these things were strange to him, and most of them amazed him greatly, and some, he thought, were silly, and laughed so hard and loud that Emmie thought surely the Beckers would be roused and think that something was the matter. She finally fell asleep, and when she was awakened by the voices in the next room, she found that Luke had not slept in the bed, but was curled up in a corner on the floor. She woke him gently, without startling him, and he sat quietly, watching her as she washed her hands and face and combed her beautiful long blond hair. She had taken to tying her hair back with a thong to keep it out of her way while working, but this morning, as she knew it would please him, she let it hang loose about her shoulders. He whispered "My Princess," into her ear as they went together to the main room and joined the Beckers, who were already eating breakfast.

Mrs. Becker greeted Emmie with "Good Morning,

Princess," and Luke wondered how she knew that Emmie was his Princess. He managed well with his utensils, and seemed very much at ease, chatting freely with Mrs. Becker as he ate. Eating was always a silent time with the Indians, and Emmie had not tried to change that habit after she and Luke had married. After the hearty meal, Emmie and Luke accompanied Mr. Becker into the post, and he appraised their bales of skins and furs. Because of the stormy hard winter, the hunters and trappers had not had a very bountiful season, and once again Mr. Becker was very pleased at the cargo they had brought to him. Luke's process of curing and tanning the skins was far superior to any white man's, and thus the quality of their furs brought a much higher price, and this he was most willing to share with them. He and Mrs. Becker had taken a great liking to Emmie; she seemed to be a part of them, even though they had known her only for a few days the year before. And now, meeting Luke, they took an immediate liking to him. Mr. Becker had never quite trusted any redskin, and had not really been too fair in some of his dealings with them. But Luke seemed somehow different. His skin being the only revealing feature of his ancestors, and it was quite obvious to any onlooker that he cared very deeply for Emmie, and she for him.

Emmie's head for business thoroughly amazed him, and he respected her greatly for it. Emmie had used one of her precious pieces of paper to draw up a list of things that they would like, and that she thought they could transport back to their home. This list she gave to Mr. Becker for him to go over and decide what they could afford. Although Emmie seemingly let Mr.

Becker make the decisions, she had already figured out that their credit from the year before would more than cover the items she had listed, and that whatever they received from their cargo this year could be added to the remainder, and their account would remain a tidy sum. This could continue to grow as the seasons unfolded, and then, of course, there was always a chance of a poor season, and they would have something in reserve to fall back upon. An iron-bladed plow, harrow and shovel had been near the top of the list, and Mr. Becker smiled as he read through the items. Almost every item was something that would benefit them in their work on the little farm. Nothing frivolous, as Mr. Becker noted, was found on the list, but which he had found on many of the lists he was requested to fill by other of his customers. Emmie had listed several kinds of seeds which he carefully weighed out and packaged and labeled. He could tell that Emmie was planning a large vegetable garden. An iron pot and and iron pan were the only items she requested to lighten her own household chores.

In the evening they sat, after the meal had been cleared away, and talked of general news that the Beckers had gathered from the trappers and farmers who had come to the post to trade their products. They told Emmie that they had inquired many times of men who were traveling from the east, and it was not until a week before that they had found someone who had known of her family. The fire, they learned, had evidently been started by a bolt of lightening, and had burned north to the river, encompassing a relatively narrow strip of land and forest. Theirs had been the only farm lost in the blaze, and when her father and brothers had returned and found the charred remains of her mother and their buildings, they had assumed that Emmie had died in the fire also, and being very crushed and despondent by what they had found and assumed, they had returned down the river and taken a ship from the port at Albany, and no one knew where they had gone. Emmie was saddened beyond words at this news. She dreamed less often of being rescued by Papa and the boys. She would not have left with them now if they had found where she was, and had come for her. Her life was now with Luke, but to think that now she could dream no longer of them finding her, and seeing how happy she was, brought sadness to her heart. Yet, tears did not come to her eyes, and so she shut the door forever on that part of her life.

Emmie induced Luke to sleep in the bed beside her that night, and they rested well, rising before the sun to prepare for the trip back to the mountains. As a special gift for Violet, Emmie chose some red glass beads that she knew Violet would cherish, and had Mr. Becker add them to their packages. The Indians had only clay and bone beads, and the transparency of the glass would surely fascinate her. The mule was nearly buried beneath the load, and even each of their horses carried part of the cargo that they had purchased. Emmie longed for many things for herself and her little cabin, but knew the impossibility of transporting such things up the hills to the little farm.

The waters had receded greatly in the short time that they had been at the post, and so they were able to follow the river to the Swenson farm, and Luke was able to meet Emmie's friends. He and George took to each other immediately, but Luke, to Emmie's amazement, was absolutely fascinated by Jon. He had grown taller since Emmie's first visit, and talked freely to Luke. Jon showed Luke a bow he had made from a sapling, and Luke taught him how to use it correctly, and how to secure a piece of flint to one end of a stick, and feathers at the other end to make a true arrrow. They would have like to stay and chat longer with the Swensons, but wanted to be above the falls on drier ground by nightfall, and so, after enjoying large mugs of refreshing tea and some of Maria's heavenly sugar cookies, they were once again on their way.

They were tired when they reached the cabin, not having slept much the night before. They had just gotten settled when it started to rain, and although the shower was not hard, nor did it last long, it was just enough to get everything wet and turned their fire into a smudge pot. Their cargo had gotten soaked, making the animals' loads much heavier, and the last leg of the trip had been hard indeed. Violet was glad to see them, and had supper ready. Emmie was delighted to find that Violet had kept very busy during their absence, and the cabin was spotless and everything was in order. They unloaded the horses and the mule, and turned them out to pasture, but they waited until morning to open the bundles and sort out their treasures. As soon as they had finished the fine meal that Violet had prepared, they climbed to their loft, soft with fresh boughs, and were quickly alseep.

It was raining in the morning, so they spent the time until noon, sorting through their purchases and showing off their new tools to Violet. She seemed pleased with all the things that were supposed to make life easier, but was utterly fascinated with the plates, knives and forks. No one but a brave was allowed a knife at the compound, and she had been surprised, to say the least, that Luke had given his precious knife to Emmie, even though he now had another, even better one, and now there was to be a knife for everyone. And these things called forks. How could they help one to eat, she asked? And so, Luke took this opportunity to show off the new way of eating he had learned while they had been at the post in the valley. Violet watched very closely and declared that the whole process seemed very silly to her, and she was sure she would never be able to master the art of eating with these strange tools. She was very taken with the string of red beads they had brought for her, and thereafter was never without them about her neck.

Chapter XIV

The spring planting went well, and it was decided that they would clear another field. With the axe and Mule to help pull logs, the task would not be nearly as hard as it had been without them. They would plant the wheat in the new field, and with fortune on their side, they could add the grain to their sale items and help build their reserve against any lean years that might be in their future.

The clearing went well, and the land was soon ready for the precious seeds. They all worked diligently, and the seed was soon in the ground. With all this work behind them, Luke set about enlarging the animal shed, and enclosing it further so the animals would be more protected in the winter months. He also planned a coop-like affair in the corner of the enlarged shed for Emmie's hens. Having to bring them inside last winter had seemed to distress Emmie greatly, and this spring one had hatched a brood of five, and so they too needed more room. Emmie and Violet busied themselves with fishing and gathering herbs and berries. Violet was a great help to Emmie, as she had been taught from infancy the ways of the Indians, and knew much more about the forest and its products than Emmie, and they gathered great baskets of roots and leaves. Violet showed Emmie how the tender leaves of the strawberries and blackberries could be used fresh or dried, and when steeped in boiling water, made delicious tea. She also showed Emmie how, when the fish that they caught were wrapped in the leaves from the wild grape vines and baked, it changed their flavor completely. Emmie was delighted at learning all these ways of using all these wonders of nature, and every night she made notes about what she had learned, and soon had many pages of notes and recipes.

They soon found that all their baskets and bowls were full, and they turned their energies to making clothes for the winter. Luke had finished the animal enclosures and had a secret project underway in the woods. He had instructed Emmie and Violet not to come where he was working, and would only smile when Emmie teased to know more about his project.

It was nearly time for harvesting their crops. The

corn stood tall, making eerie shadows in the moonlight, and Emmie's small vegetable garden had thrived under her tender care. The morning dawned bright and clear, and after they had eaten breakfast, Luke left for the woods, but whispered to Violet before he left. Emmie could not understand his abruptness, but went about her chores and went to the clearing downstream to gather some tall grasses for basket weaving. Violet stayed behind, busying herself with gathering fresh boughs for her mat. Emmie thought this rather strange, as Violet rarely stayed behind alone, but she went on and was soon engrossed in her work, carefully selecting the tallest grasses and reeds, piling them by the path. She wandered further, and then found a patch of wild oats, and decided to take the grasses she had ready back to the cabin and get Violet and a sack and return for the oats. The grain was very ripe and they would be able to shake the kernels directly onto a large mat, without having to cut and stack them today. And so she retraced her steps back to the cabin, noting in her mind where the find was. When she arrived back at the cabin, the sun was high in the sky, and she wondered if Violet had prepared anything for the noon meal. If not, and if Luke had not returned, they would take some biscuits and smoked fish with them and picnic on the way. No one seemed to be there as she approached, and she felt a little perturbed at being so deserted, but when she entered the cabin, she was greeted by the surprise that Luke had been so secretive about. He had made them a table and a chair for each of them. Even since their trip to the post, he had talked about the furnishings at Mrs. Becker's, and had found the new eating utensils hard to manage on his lap as he sat cross-legged on the floor. Emmie was so taken back with the surprise that she was speechless, and for a few moments Luke thought she was not pleased. But she soon recovered her voice, and he could tell from both her words and facial expressions that she was greatly pleased. It was what he had whispered to Violet in the morning, and as soon as Emmie had left, she had set about preparing a fine stew for them, and so, sitting in their new chairs around their new table, they ate heartily from the new plates and knives and forks.

The afternoon was nearly spent when they had finished their meal and washed the dishes, and so, after telling Luke and Violet of her find, it was decided that they would go in the morning and harvest the grain. They would take Mule, havest the oats, cut and bundle the straw, then bring that back, for use during the winter instead of boughs for bedding for the animals. Emmie was up early and packed a lunch for them, and as soon as the chores were finished, they were off. The project was greater than Emmie had thought, and they had to return a second day to gather all the straw. Luke was pleased at her find, and was proud of the great stack of straw, and immediately started a lean-to to protect it from the fall rains and winter snow. When the snows finally came, they had finished their harvesting, and had every nook and corner crammed with supplies for the long, cold winter ahead.

Emmie was always sad when Luke started out to hunt and tend his trap lines, but she and Violet managed to keep warm and busy in the little cabin. Violet was an apt student, and soon could read and write nearly as well as Emmie. Emmie tried to explain about God and what they read from her Bible, and although both Luke and Violet seemed to enjoy the tales she told, they clung to their own religious beliefs, praying to their own Great Spirit as they had been taught since early childhood. As the sun rose higher each day, and the days grew longer, Emmie started her list for Mr. Becker. Luke had been very successful on his hunting trips, and their bales of furs and hides would be many. Violet hinted at wanting to go to the post with them, but someone must stay behind and tend to the daily chores. So it was with reluctance that she saw Emmie and Luke off on the first warm day of spring. As they rode past their new wheat field, the first tiny green sprouts of the wheat were peeping through the ground.

The Swensons were glad to see them, and George and Luke went directly to the barn to see a calf that had been born just a day or two before. Maria's body was much rounder than it had been last year, and she explained that she would have a baby any day now. Emmie was elated over Maria's news. She would like a baby too, she confided to Maria, but that blessing seemed to have passed them by. Being thoroughly refreshed, they were soon on their way and made the post well before nightfall. Both Mr. and Mrs. Becker were on hand to greet them, although Mrs. Becker told Emmie that she hadn't expected them for another week or so. The first thing the next morning, Mr. Becker showed Emmie and Luke about. He had expanded the post, and had many more supplies to offer than before. Both were impressed, but Luke left all the decisions to Emmie, and she held closely to the list that she had spent so many hours preparing. Mr. Becker inquired about the wheat seeds Emmie had taken the spring before, and was anxious about the expected abundance of the crop. He suggested that if possible, she try and get the grain to him directly after harvest, and promised her top price if she could. Emmie put this suggestion from her mind, as not being practical for them, and did not tell Luke of the suggestion Mr. Becker had made.

The goods selected and loaded, they stayed but two nights, and were off with the sunrise on the second morning. Mrs. Becker hated to see them go so soon. She had hardly time for visiting, and Emmie was one of the few white women that came to the post, but she felt that she could not urge them to stay, for she knew of the many tasks that lay ahead for them. When they arrived back at the Swenson farm, Jon greeted them with the news that the new baby had arrived, a girl they would call Ellen. Emmie hurried in to see Maria and the child, and Luke went to the barn for a quick visit with George. They had tea, with biscuits, and were quickly on their way agian. With the exception of Emmie's quietness, the trip back to the little farm was uneventful. Luke guessed that Emmie's quietness had to do with the Swenson's new baby. He was not too keen on a girl-child as this one was, but would be pleased indeed for a son like Jon. Perhaps, he thought, someday the Great Spirit would so bless them, and then their happiness would be complete.

Plowing and planting awaited them upon their return, and they were soon busy with the extra chores of the spring. Violet was especially glad to see them, and told them that a young brave from the compound had stopped while they had been gone. He brought much news of her home people, telling of marriages, births and deaths. They were glad of the news, although Emmie was most upset to hear that the old squaw who had nursed her back to health when Luke had found her, and had taken her to the compound, and had watched over her so carefully before her marriage to Luke, was among those who had passed away. They must not wait so long to visit, she told Luke. Too many changes took place, and they must keep in touch with his kinfolk. He promised her a trip after the planting was finished.

Emmie worked far into the night, using the flames of the fire as her light, making up the new material she had bought from Mr. Becker, to make a dress for the expected trip. The material had an overall pattern, but the background was light blue, the same shade as her eyes, and she wanted it to be perfect. She made an apron-like affair to match, and felt it was very elegant when it was finished. Luke was very pleased with her efforts, and was indeed proud of her when they arrived at the compound. They quickly learned that the brave who had visited in their absence in the spring wanted Violet for his wife, and made no hesitation in seeking Luke's consent. It was soon decided that Luke would take two of the younger braves and ride back to the farm for Violet, and the boys would stay there and tend to chores until they returned.

Violet arrived, looking anything but the happy bride-to-be, and Luke quickly related the problem to Emmie. Violet did not want to come back to the compound to live, and she had made it very clear to him that she would be most unhappy if he insisted she go through with the marriage, and he now asked Emmie's advice. She quickly offered the solution, and it was acceptable to all. The newly-weds would return to the farm with them. It was but right that Violet have a husband, and it was apparent to all that she was in love with this young brave. But Emmie understood, more than the men, of Violet's desires to live like she and Luke. They had had her with them for several years now, and had taught her of the white man's ways, and she did not wish to return to the hard life of her ancestors.

The young brave's name was like all other Indian names, long and difficult for the white man to pronounce, but Luke had taught Emmie the meaning of many of these names, and she interpreted the groom's name to mean "builder," and once again, referring to her Christian training, she decided to call him "Joseph." Violet and Luke were both pleased, and so with the bridegroom's approval, he became "Joseph." The Chief was agreeable to the plan, and so, as soon as the ceremony and celebration were over, they all returned down the hills to the farm. Joseph's presence would lighten Emmie's work in the fields, and Violet's happiness would be assured.

Another small room was added to the cabin, and Joseph and Violet settled quickly to married life. The wheat was then ready and the harvest was begun. The crop seemed plentiful, and it was as they reaped the fruits of their crop that Emmie told Luke of Mr. Becker's request to bring the grain to the post as soon as it was harvested, and so it was quickly decided that Luke would be the one to make the trip. Emmie would stay and oversee the work that must be done. Emmie quickly made a soft fur robe for the Swenson's new baby, and a warm parka for Jon, and packed them in one of her most beautiful baskets for Luke to deliver on his way.

Luke made the trip in half the time it had taken them before, and when he returned, he had two folded pieces of paper for Emmie. One from Mr. Becker, informing her of the amount he had credited to her account for the grain, and the amount pleased her greatly. She told Joseph and Violet that this amount they would share with them, and that they could prepare a list of things they would like brought back to them in the spring. The second paper contained a note from Maria. She told of the baby's progress, and thanked Emmie for the fine gifts she had sent. Emmie read and reread the note. This was the first letter Emmie had ever received, and she carefully stowed it away with her meager treasures.

The little farm thrived under Emmie and Luke's direction, and the trips to the post became both spring and fall events for several years. Violet and Joseph now had a baby girl. Violet never left the infant alone, carrying her with her at all times in a basket she strapped to her shoulders. Emmie offered many times to stay at the cabin and watch her, but Violet refused any assistance with the child, and Emmie smiled to herself, thinking how Indian-like, even for all her white man's ways, Violet was acting. The Indian babies were always the sole responsibility of the squaw, and Violet was taking her responsibilities very seriously. Emmie made the fall trip alone that year, and could not help but feel concern about Mr.

Becker's health. He had seemed much older, and had moved very slowly.

In the spring, when they both made the trip, Emmie's concern grew. Every movement seemed to be an effort for him. She hesitated to mention any of this to Mrs. Becker, but as soon as they were on their way again, she quickly confided her concern to Luke. He too, had noticed the change, but he dismissed her concerns, saying that Mr. Becker was no doubt working more than usual, recalling how business at the post had increased greatly in recent years, and that a restful summer should find him well again in the fall. His condition in the fall seemed to have improved ever so slightly, and they rode back up the mountain with raised hopes for the old man. However, when they returned the next spring, his condition had again worsened, and Mrs. Becker's concern was most evident. He no longer was able to manage the post alone, and she was not able to be of much help to him. She had fallen on some ice during the winter, and had developed a very noticeable limp. The two, Emmie thought, presented a very sad picture, indeed.

Emmie and Luke's account had grown steadily over the years, and was equal, Mrs. Becker thought, to the entire stock of the post, and as she related her troubles to Emmie and Luke, a plan was forming in her mind. Would they be willing to leave their farm and come and take over the post? It was a big decision for them to make, and they should not decide in a hurry. They had worked hard to build up their little farm, and had, but two years before, filled out papers for the government offices to make the land legally theirs.

Luke had not understood all this paper work and the legal terms, but had done as the Becker's suggested, and their application for the land had been granted. Luke's ancestors had always ruled over the mountains, and he had never thought of the land belonging to anyone else.
   They slept very little that night, discussing for hours Mrs. Becker's proposal. Neither was sure that leaving their precious farm would be the right thing, but in the morning, while Luke was overseeing the packing and loading of the cargo, Mrs. Becker told Emmie of the word from down the valley of the plans for a canal that was to be built through the valley, and this news was the swaying point in their decision. They would go back up to the farm with the supplies that had been bargained for, and discuss plans with Joseph and Violet, and if all was agreeable with them, they would plan to stay at least until the winter, when they would return on their annual fall trip. They had all heard many times of great plans for a canal, but with the fall of Mr. Clinton from power, they had assumed all these plans had been scrapped. There had been a company formed some years previously, The Lock Navigation Company, that had not been successful in its endeavor to build a waterway for boats around the carry at Little Falls, and the failure of this company had not helped Mr. Clinton's cause. But rumor had risen again, and Mr. Clinton was once again being heard from.
   They chatted of nothing else on the way home. They stopped at the Swenson's, and had some refreshments, but told neither Maria or George of Mrs. Becker's proposition. After they were on their

way, Maria spoke to George about their anxiety, and fretted that they had a problem.

When they arrived home, Jospeh and Violet greeted them warmly, and while the men unloaded the animals, Violet told Emmie that she was expecting a second child in the early fall, and she was delighted, and so Emmie delayed her news of Mrs. Becker's offer until she had a chance to talk with Luke. Although she was delighted at Violet's news, she wondered if she should let it interfere with their decision to leave. It was not until they had retired for the night that she had a chance to visit alone with him about the expected child. They decided to leave the decision up to Violet and Joseph, and so, directly after morning chores, when they were all working at unpacking, they informed them of their plans. Violet was sure she could manage alone. After all, Teka was nearly seven years old and would be a great help to her, and would be fine company for her when Jospeh was away in the winter. And so, it was decided that after the baby was born in the fall, and the harvest was finished, Luke and Emmie would leave to spend the winter with Mr. and Mrs. Becker at the post.

They were all kept busy during the summer, gathering and drying supplies for the winter, and after the wood piles were high with more than enough fuel to see them through the winter, Joseph spent his leisure time making a cradle for the baby, and Emmie worked at stitching tiny booties and socks, decorating them with bits of ribbons and colored cloth that had accumulated in her sewing basket. When Violet's time came, all was in readiness, and all went well. Violet's labor was not long, and the baby was a healthy boy. Joseph and Violet had already decided to name him after Luke if it was a boy, and so he was immediately called "Little Luke."

Emmie had long ago decided what she would take with her, and had carefully packed her treasures in a large deerskin sack, ready for the trip to the valley. Luke was not taking many things with him, leaving behind all his precious tools for Joseph. He looked longingly at his axe, worn thin now from use through these many years, and recalled vividly to his mind the emotion he had felt when Emmie had brought it to him after her first trip to the post. He decided to take it with him. Joseph had a new one now, and there were too many memories connected with it that couldn't be left behind. He strapped it to the waiting pack, and so it was that in the fall of 1817 Emmie and Luke set out, down their mountain to embark on a new adventure.

Chapter XV

They rode leisurely down the now well-known trail. Emmie drinking in and storing in her memories every ounce of all she held dear. The meadow where she had discovered the wild oats; the cove where she and Violet came so often to bathe; passing the clearing where she and Ebony had camped on her first trip down the mountain, brought tears to her eyes. They forged on, even after the sun began to set. Their loads were light, and the trail well marked, and when the moon rose, full and bright, they decided to continue to ride on.

They were not in any particular hurry, but had no desire to prolong their leaving any longer than absolutely necessary. The swamps were dry, as the fall rains had not yet begun, and after they had gotten around the falls, they crossed the marshes and arrived at the Swenson's just as George and Jon, now a tall young man, were walking to the barn for morning chores. Luke went with the men, and Emmie went to the friendly farm kitchen to join Maria, where the aroma of smoked pork and griddle cakes met her. Ellen was setting the table, and quickly added two places for them. Emmie never ceased to be amazed at how grown-up Ellen seemed, more so even now than just last spring. By the time breakfast was ready, the men were in from the barn and had washed up. The chatter at breakfast covered everything that happened to each other over the summer months, and then Emmie told them of their plans to help the Beckers at the post, and that their plans for the future would depend on Mr. Becker's health. George offered that he had heard just last week from a man travelling west that the post had been tended by an old lady and a squaw. Upon hearing this news, Emmie and Luke quickly bid the Swensons good-bye, and rode rapidly to the post, arriving to find it closed, and the door barred. They quickly ran around to the back and entered the kitchen and found Mrs. Becker's faithful squaw sitting alone. Without rising, or even looking up, she told them of Mr. Becker's death, and that he had been buried just yesterday. Bidding Luke to go outside and find the old hunch-back, and tend the horses, Emmie hurried to the front room to find Mrs. Becker, and when she was not there, she went to the bedroom and found that she was still in bed.

Rising on one arm, she bid Emmie to sit beside her. Emmie could tell from her voice that the old lady was exhausted. She left to return shortly with some hot coffee and biscuits, with wild apple jelly. Mrs. Becker ate in silence, and after she had finished the last crumb, she threw her arms around Emmie and welcomed her "Princess." They talked for hours, Mrs. Becker going over her life with Mr. Becker from the time of the raid until yesterday, when she had laid him to rest beneath the oak tree, just to the west of the post. When she had finished, Emmie helped her up, and slipping a robe about her shoulders, led her to the living room, where Luke now waited for them. They talked quietly for hours, being interrupted only by the ebbing strength of Mrs. Becker.

It was finally settled that Emmie and Luke would reopen the post in the morning, and so they all retired early and slept as though drugged. The long trip without rest, and the sad news that greeted them on their arrival had completely exhausted both of them. But after a good night's rest, they were up at dawn and ready for a busy day of trading.

Traffic was steady. Trappers and hunters buying supplies for the coming winter, and a few farmers trading grain and produce for family necessities and new tools. They were so busy that there had been no time to take a counting of the supplies on hand, and so Emmie had started her own book, leaving the one Mr. Becker had used untouched. These Emmie would go over later with Mrs. Becker.

They had been operating the post but a few days when a group of men stopped, wanting lodging. There were no rooms at the post that could accomodate them, but Luke told them they could camp in the clearing behind the post if this would help them. During the conversation that ensued, it was learned that they were surveyors, and were on their way to Albany with the final maps for the canal. And so, Emmie thought, this great waterway was to be a reality, and would, she was sure, change the way of life in the valley.

All during the long winter, Emmie and Luke made plans. With Mr. Becker gone, there seemed to be no question but that they would remain in the valley and take over the post. Supplies had been ordered from Albany, and New York before Mr. Becker's death, and these supplies started to arrive even before the first signs of spring. And long before all that had been ordered had arrived, they had run out of storage space. Mr. Becker had had news of the canal, and with his uncanny foresight, had more than doubled his usual orders for shovels, axes, heavy boots and blankets.

While Emmie and Luke were in the living room late one evening, Mrs. Becker came in and sat in her rocking chair by the fire. Her health had greatly improved over the long winter, and although she still walked with a noticeable limp from the nasty fall the previous winter, and now used a stick for better balance, her general health was very good. She interrupted the conversation and asked them to listen to her for a moment or two. They complied in amazement. She had given them a free hand in running the post, and it was now in great wonderment that they waited for her to speak.

She could see, she said, that in the short time they had been there, that the post would flourish under their management. Emmie's head for figures, and Luke's knowledge of skins and furs, and his ability to deal with both the white man and the Indians, was an unbeatable combination. She had tired of all this, and although she loves "her Princess" as the daughter she never had, she wanted to leave. She longed to see her brother and sisters; that although she had heard from them on occasion through the years, she had not actually seen them since she left home as a bride, well over 40 years before, and there were nieces and nephews that she knew only by name. She had thought about this plan for some time, and felt that now was the time to carry through with it. She held on her lap a metal box which she opened with a large key, and withdrew a paper that she had drawn up, and slowly read it to them. Its contents were quite detailed. She was giving all her rights of the post to them. She was asking only that when the time came, she could return and be laid to rest beside Mr. Becker under the great oak tree. She would, she stated, have a legal deed to the post drawn up for them upon her arrival at the courthouse in Herkimer, and send it by a reliable courier back to them. She replaced the paper in the box, and gave the key to Emmie. In the morning, Luke informed the old hunch-back of the change of ownership, and asked him to stay on, and he readily agreed. But when Emmie talked to the squaw, she wept openly, and declared that she must go with Mrs. Becker and look after her. These arrangements were agreed upon, and the packing of the few personal items that the ladies would take with them was underway. A farmer, travelling east in a crude, open wagon, agreed to take them along to Deerfield, where they would find accomodations until they could book passage on a stage to Herkimer and then to Albany.

Although they worked with heavy hearts, Emmie and Luke were too busy and too tired at the day's end to lament on their sadness and the void, left in their lives by Mrs. Becker's departure. Emmie found that she had little time for cooking and housekeeping with the squaw gone, and there was no one to help her with any of these chores. She soon found herself in a turmoil. She had not been solely responsible for any of these chores for many years, and now found, it seemed, impossible to keep up with them. Luke could see that the situation was overcoming her and suggested that she ride to the Swenson's and see if perhaps Ellen, although she was very young, would not come and live with them, if only for the summer months, or until they could find someone to take over these chores for Emmie.

It was a bright and sunny spring morning, and Emmie decided that although there was much to be done at the post, she could no longer do without help in the house, and so she set off to visit her dearest friend, Maria Swenson, and ask for her daughter.

The ride was a pleasant one, and although Ebony was very old, having outlived by many years the normal age of a horse, his pace was spry and they made good time. She passed many riders on the way, as well as wagons, and could see several settlers on the south side of the river, and she thought of her first ride through this valley, and how the Swensons were the only settlers between the post and the brook that led up to the falls and on up the mountain. She spotted George and Jon setting posts for a new fence in their east pasture, and waved at them. When she arrived at the house, she found Ellen hanging out a washing, and a feeling of guilt swept over her for even thinking of asking Maria for this child, but consoled herself with the thought that the plan was only temporary. She dismounted and threw her reins over the hitching post and entered the kitchen. Maria was delighted at this unexpected visit, and immediately put on a kettle for tea, and her questions about Luke, the post and news from down river came so fast that Emmie didn't even try to interrupt her for several minutes. She tried to sort out the questions, and answer them one at a time. The women chatted for some time, Ellen joining them when she had finished her laundry chores, and Emmie thought how like her mother Ellen was. The same slim beauty that Maria had been when she had stopped those many years before, a tired, frightened girl on her first trip to the post.

When Maria's thirst for news had been satisfied, Emmie told her of the reason for her visit. When she had finished, they both looked at Ellen, whose face, they found, was a picture of excitement. Please, could she go with Emmie, she begged her mother, and although Maria felt saddened by the girl's desire to leave, knew that it would be a rewarding experience for her, and that Emmie and Luke would take good care of her. But she must wait for George to come in before she could make such a decision. It was nearly suppertime, and the three busied themselves with preparing the meal, and when they heard George and

Jon return from the pasture where they had waved at Emmie, Maria slipped quickly out and met them. The two left behind grew silent, and both wondered what the decision would be. Jon came in first and teasingly pulled his sister's hair, and said that he had heard that she was a big girl now. He quickly washed up and was ready for supper when George and Maria came in. George greeted Emmie, and spoke of seeing her ride by earlier in the day, and try as she did, she could not detect from his voice or expression, what his reaction to her request was going to be.

George sat down at the table, and offered a long blessing, thoughtfully including Emmie in his prayer, and it was not until the meal was finished, and the food cleared away, that he spoke to Emmie of her request to take Ellen back to the post with her. He realized, he said, how very busy she and Luke must be; he appreciated that she needed help, and because they had been friends for so long, they would let them "borrow" Ellen on a trial basis for the summer. There could be no talk of wages, as they could under no circumstances accept money from friends, but she and Luke could be responsible if Ellen needed anything while she was with them. And so, before they slept, arrangements were made to pack Ellen's few necessities, and be ready to ride to the post with Emmie the next morning. George would let them take one of his horses for Ellen to ride as Ebony was much too old to be expected to carry both of them, and he or Jon would be by in a week or two for some supplies and pick up the animal then.

They rode in silence for some time. Emmie feeling it best to let Ellen start the conversation. She knew the girl had never been away from her home before, and that this was the biggest event to occur in her young life, so Emmie did not want to make light conversation at this time. They were nearly to the post before Ellen spoke, and she was very serious when she asked Emmie to outline the duties that would be expected of her. Emmie explained that she would leave the house entirely up to her. She could arrange the chores as she saw fit, and although it probably sounded like an enormous undertaking for one so young, Emmie assured her that outside of a hearty meal in the evening, for which she would even leave the menu up to her, her duties would be few. Ellen was pleased that the decisions about the meals would be left up to her, because she enjoyed cooking.

There were several men at the post, so Emmie took the long path to avoid the roving eyes and the remarks that were sure to be directed at them, and she did not want Ellen frightened before they had even arrived. When they entered the kitchen, Ellen stood in awe. She had never seen any of the equipment that she now was confronted with. An iron stove! They had only a fireplace with a swinging crane, and a brick oven in their kitchen at home, and she couldn't believe her eyes at the array of cooking utensils and pots and pans. How, she thought, would she ever manage in so grand a kitchen?

Emmie and Luke had kept the little bedroom for themselves, even after Mrs. Becker had left. Luke said he would feel more comfortable in the little room, and so the big room that had been Mrs. Becker's, was now readied for Ellen. When Emmie showed her the room, great tears rolled down her cheeks. She had all her life shared the loft at home with Jon. They each had their own side, with a curtain between, but their beds were small and the loft had a low ceiling, and this great bed seemed to overcome her. Emmie tried to make light of it all, but was remembering her first trip to the post, and all the awe and wonder she had felt then. Ellen walked around and around the room, first just looking and then picking up and examining all of the things that were so new to her.

Luke came in and was delighted to see them, and was glad that the Swensons had allowed Ellen to come back with Emmie. He could see that the girl was awestruck, and suggested to Emmie that they have a little lunch, thinking that perhaps Ellen would like to be alone for a little while, but she quickly laid down her small sack of possessions on the bed and joined them back in the kitchen. As they ate, Ellen became more relaxed, and chatted freely with them about her new surroundings. She was so anxious to learn about everything that she saw, that Emmie became worried that she was getting too excited. Her face was flushed, and her voice became almost shrill. And so, after they ate, Emmie suggested that perhaps she would like to get settled in her new room and rest for a short while before taking on any of the chores, as there was nothing so pressing that it couldn't wait. Ellen reluctantly agreed, but found that she could not rest, and so, instead, joined Emmie and Luke in the post. She was even more surprised at the store than the house, and as soon as Emmie was free for a moment, she took her back inside and showed her the household supply cupboards, and suggested, that perhaps she could bake some cookies, or perhaps some corn bread for supper. To help her, this first day, Emmie made her a list of what she might prepare for supper, and after instructing her in the use of the stove, left her alone and returned to the post. There were many traders throughout the afternoon, many making camp in the grove at the rear of the building. Having to travel such long distances, that both men and animals needed much rest before a return trip.

Ellen talked incessantly throughout the evening meal, asking repeatedly if everything was all right. Having been so overcome with the great quantities in the supply cupboards, she had baked all afternoon, and they were literally overcome with cookies and breads. But the girl certainly had a way with "vittles" (a new word for Luke), and both he and Emmie were pleased at her first day's accomplishments. Emmie offered to help with the clearing up, but Ellen wouldn't accept her offer, and so she sat at the table and chatted with her, keeping her company until the room was spotless. While chatting with Emmie, Ellen wished aloud that Mama could see her now, and that she could hardly wait for Papa to come for the horse so she could tell him all about the house and furnishings.

The first thing in the morning, before breakfast, Emmie went into the post and returned with a box of paper and a pen, a bottle of ink and a stand, and told Ellen they were for her, and that every day she could write down about her life here at the post, and when her Papa came, she could send the writings to her Mama. A sort of daily letter, then they would know all about her and what she was doing. Ellen was delighted with the idea. She had never written on paper with a pen and ink before, she confessed to Emmie, telling her that she had only had a slate and pencil at home. So Emmie showed her, explaining not to get too much ink on the pen or she would make splotches. Ellen learned quickly, and after breakfast, when Emmie and Luke went into the post to open for the day's business, they left Ellen sitting at the kitchen table, writing away. But when she peeked in a short time later, she found the room spotless, and a great kettle of venison stewing away on the back of the stove. Emmie was delighted and very pleased as she knew that Luke's idea to bring the girl here would work out just fine.

The summer passed rapidly. The river and trails all busy with boats and wagons, hauling canal workers and their families to the great project. News always was concerned with the progress of the canal, and how great it would be when completed, connecting the western rivers and lakes with the great ocean. Many of the workers had been brought across the great ocean to work on the canal, and Emmie thought them a happy, friendly lot, and their demands were few. Even so, supplies at the post ran dangerously low by early fall, and Emmie doubled all their orders for spring. The harvest was plentiful that fall, but Emmie and Luke had little left to send down the valley as the canalers used up their supplies nearly as fast as the farmers brought them in.

Emmie thrived on all the work that was required of her to keep the books and inventory up to date. To better suit her personal attire to her duties, she wore almost entirely her Indian dresses, finding them less constricting than the floor-length, full skirts and many petticoats that were the fashion of the day, and she had taken to braiding her long golden hair, and winding it around her head, and the braids formed, without her realizing it, a sort of halo or crown, and she looked to Luke like a picture in one of the books Mrs. Becker had left behind, of a princess, and he knew now what she had meant when he had first heard her call Emmie her "Adirondack Princess."

A rider came through in early fall, who asked to speak privately with Emmie, and so she invited him to the house kitchen and called to Ellen to please put on the coffee pot, and bring some of her special molasses cookies. He had ridden from Albany, he said, and had news of Mrs. Becker, and a package from her for Emmie, which he took from the inside of his shirt. Emmie put it unopened on the mantel shelf, as she was anxious for the news of Mrs. Becker. She was with a niece, her sister's oldest girl, in Albany, and had bade him tell Emmie how well and happy she was. The niece, he told Emmie, was alone, having lost her husband in the recent war (1812), and so they were company for each other. She asked Emmie to write to her with news of the post and the progress of the canal project. The traveller thanked Emmie for her hospitality, but said he must be on his way, as he had letters from the Albany headquarters for the canal boss on to the west, and hoped to reach him before nightfall.

It was not until after the evening meal, and she was preparing for bed, that Emmie remembered the package the messenger had brought her. She quickly tore it open and found a letter for herself and a small package for Luke. Emmie opened her letter carefully, and found not a letter, but the legal paper that Mrs. Becker had promised her, making the post legally theirs. Emmie carefully folded the document, and placed it in the tin box that Mrs. Becker had left with her. This done, she turned to Luke to see what was in the package that had been marked for him, but the package was nowhere in sight, and the broad smile on his face told Emmie that it contained some sort of surprise for her, and no amount of teasing would make him divulge that secret until he was ready.

After harvest that fall, Maria and George left Jon in charge at home, and came to the post for a visit. Maria had not seen her daughter since that day in the spring when she had come to the post to help Emmie. Ellen had faithfully written down all that had gone on in her life here at the post, and had made very realistic sketches of all the furnishings and equipment that was so new and exciting to her, and had sent these pictures and stories with travellers going west to her mother at every opportunity, and Maria had enjoyed them very much. Especially the one of Ellen, surrounded by pots and pans, in front of the great iron stove, with the table in the background, laden with cakes and breads. But she still longed to see Ellen in the flesh, and to make plans for her future. She and George had only agreed to her staying for the summer, and the busy fall season. But Maria was sure that it would be a mistake to take Ellen back to the farm now. She felt in her heart that once having experienced life at the post, and in Luke and Emmie's lovely home, that the girl would be very unhappy back with them.

The reunion was a happy one, and Maria could see at once that Ellen had matured greatly in the short time she had been away. With material that Emmie had given her, she had made herself a new dress, and Maria knew from the figure revealed by the new, close-fitting garment, that her daughter was now a young lady. Ellen wanted to stay on with Emmie and Luke, but said she would, of course, respect her parents' wishes. She retired early that night, but not to the grand bedroom where she had slept these many months she had been there. She had insisted that she sleep on a cot-like affair that she had arranged behind the kitchen stove, and that her parents share the great bed. As she lay on her little cot, sleep did not come easy. The excitement of seeing her mother for the first time in so long, and the fact that her whole future was at this moment being decided on the other side of the partition, made sleeping almost impossible.

She arose before dawn, and urging the coals in the great stove to a crimson glow, she silently set about preparing a hearty breakfast. By the time the others had begun to stir, the aromas emitting from the kitchen were delightful indeed. With breakfast over, the men went into the post to open for the day's business, but Emmie stayed behind with Maria to tell Ellen of the decision that had been reached about her future. She could stay, and the conditions upon this decision were few. The most important one being that Emmie and Luke must further her education. She could read and write well, but had little or no knowledge of arithmetic. She could count and knew how to distinguish one number from another, but had no idea of sums or values, and these things Emmie had agreed to teach her. So much had been available to her here at the post that Maria and George wanted to be sure that she did not lose sight of the value of these material things. Should she marry and have a household of her own to manage, this training, they felt, would be very necessary. And so, with these arrangements made, and George's business at the post concluded, they returned to their farm.

Chapter XVI

Work on the canal, although slowed by the cold and snow, continued throughout the winter, and made the usual slow time at the post pass much more rapidly. As the holiday season approached, Ellen longed, for the first time, for home and all the excitement that always accompanied the season. As no one spoke of the coming holiday season to her, she approached Emmie about how she and Luke planned to celebrate. Emmie was silent for a long time, remembering those happy times at home with Ma and Papa and the boys.

She recalled the tree, strung with popcorn, and hung with fancy shaped cookies; the doll Ma had made her with the scraps from her sewing basket; and the crude little bed that Papa had made for the doll; and the special dinner of wild turkey that Ma had prepared, that was always the highlight of the day. She had told these tales to Luke many times, but they had never celebrated the holiday themselves with any tree or gift-giving. After all, it was Emmie's religion, not his, and she tried not to press her beliefs upon him. But with Ellen here, Emmie decided that this year would be different, and so, axe in hand, she and Ellen set out early one morning to find just the right tree. After rejecting several along the eastern path as either too short or too tall, they found one that suited them both; one that Ellen referred to as a "plump little fellow." And so, with but a few carefully aimed swings of her axe, Emmie felled the tree and they dragged it back through the snow to the kitchen door. When Luke saw them coming down the path, he smiled broadly. The women, without their knowing it, were helping him with his secret plan.

He had known from Emmie's tales, over these many years, how much this celebration of the birthday of her God, that she prayed to so faithfully, meant to her, and he had secretly decided that it was time for him to participate in a celebration with her. He had talked it over with Mrs. Becker, and she had, as she promised, sent him the present that he would give to Emmie. And so he entered into the activities with zest, making braces to hold the tree upright in the corner of the living room, and commenting favorably and encouraging them as they made decorations and hung them on the tree. Emmie carefully selected and wrapped many items from the post for Ellen, and Ellen secretly worked at her project for them.

On Christmas Eve they lighted the candles Emmie had made and secured to the outer boughs of the tree, and they sat silently and sipped a hot, soothing toddy that Ellen had concocted of milk and eggs and rum. Just before retiring they each brought out their gifts for each other, and carefully laid them beneath the tree to be opened in the morning. None of them slept much that night.

Ellen was delighted with her gifts, which included several lengths of material from which she could fashion both outer and under garments, and her first pair of "store-bought" shoes, which she put on and declared she would never take off. Ellen's gift to them was a painting of both of them, and she had captured their likenesses well. The colors, she explained, she had made by adding fruits and berries and leaves to water, and had made the fine strokes with brushes made from feathers. They were both speechless at the great talent that the girl had displayed, and Emmie immediately hung the portrait on the wall opposite the big mirror, which reflected the painting, and it could be seen from all points in the large room. Luke kept his present for Emmie until last, knowing, he felt, that the surprise would be overwhelming. When she opened the tiny box, she ran to him and buried her face in his shoulder, and wept uncontrollably for several minutes. It was a plain gold ring like the one Mrs. Becker wore, and which had always fascinated Luke. He had asked her about it before she had left, and she had explained that it was a symbol of the love

Mr. Becker had for her, and that it was a very old custom of the white man to give such a ring to his bride when they were wed. Of course, many wives were wed and greatly loved and respected without such a symbol because gold rings were very expensive and rare in this wilderness. Luke had decided that his Princess should have such a symbol, and had asked Mrs. Becker, when she had left for Albany, that if it was possible for her to find one, to send it to him, and so he lifted the precious gold circle from its box, and slipped it on Emmie's finger, and like Ellen's shoes, she vowed she would never take it off.

Chapter XVII

With the coming of spring that year, the post bustled with activity, and the stream of traders and travellers never seemed to cease. The canal stood, a great dry ditch, on the south side of the river, the workers having moved on to other points. But word came as to the progress being made both east and west of them, and Emmie and Luke realized that when the canal opened for business, their little post would be greatly affected. They discussed these changes, and how it would affect their lives, and felt that they should make some preparations for the future. Neither had any desire to return to their mountain farm. Violet and Jospeh had enlarged the cabin as their family had grown, and they now had two sons and Teka. They were well-to-do, having each season brought to the post fine quality furs and skins and wheat to sell and trade. They were happy on the farm, and Emmie and Luke had no desire to interrupt that happiness.

There was to be a lock in the canal, almost directly in front of their post, and it was Luke's plan that they finally decided to put into action. They were on the north side of the river, and a bridge would have to be built, but his idea to enlarge the post to an Inn was exciting to Emmie, and so, long before the snows came that fall, a great pile of logs stood ready for spring construction. They hired men who no longer were needed for canal work, and the pile of logs grew all through the winter. When spring finally burst forth upon them, construction began. Emmie thought Luke's plans much too grand and elaborate for a country inn, but went along with them, her experiences of the past having taught her that he was more often right than wrong.

Construction of the Inn proceded under his guidance and the building soon rose tall among the trees. Emmie kept busy in the post, but found time for a long visit with Maria when she came with George to get their spring supplies. They were proud of Ellen's progress with her studies, and amazed at the artistic talent her drawings and paintings displayed.

When Joseph came and saw the construction that was underway, he offered to send two of the boys down to help, but Luke graciously refused his offer, knowing that he needed the boys at home to help get the spring plowing and planting done. But before he left, Emmie extracted a promise from him to bring Violet for a long-delayed visit in the fall.

As the weather grew warmer, Ellen could be found, after her household duties were finished, down by the river with her sketch pad, and it came as no great surprise to any of them when a traveller, who had stopped to rest, admired her work. But when he asked if he might purchase the picture that she had been putting the final touches on when he had arrived, they were speechless. Ellen looked at Emmie for advice, and Emmie was as much at a loss as Ellen to know what to say. The traveller quickly explained that he had a lot of influential friends in New York City, and if they would allow him to purchase the picture, he might be able to secure some orders for her from these friends. Ellen had never thought of her pictures as anything but a pleasant way to pass the time, and now this man was offering her money, and perhaps a chance to earn more money. Her pleading look told Emmie that she must decide, and so set what she thought to be a ridiculously high price, thinking he might be discouraged from buying, and Ellen would not be hurt or disappointed if he didn't send for any more, and so she told Ellen she thought one dollar would be a fair price.

Ellen was aghast. Why, that was more money than she had ever had all at once in her young life. In fact, in the little leather sack that she kept hidden in the bottom of her sewing basket held six bright copper pennies, and it was hard for her to even imagine 100 of these. But the gentleman, for surely must be a gentleman not to have fainted at the price Emmie had set, took a gleaming silver dollar from his waistcoat pocket and handed it to Ellen. He then asked to see more of her sketches, and was immediately impressed by the portrait of Emmie and Luke that hung in the living room. He had her mark her name on the lower corner of the sketch he had purchased, and then carefully rolled it up and gently eased it, so as not to crease it, in his saddle bag. He bid them farewell, stating that he wished to make Utica before nightfall, and assuring Ellen that she would hear from him, he rode off. When Emmie related the visit to Luke after the evening meal, his opinion was the same as Emmie's, and although they both enjoyed and appreciated her talents, they could hardly believe that anyone would actually buy any of the pictures.

Emmie spoke to Ellen as she set out to sketch by her favorite spot at the river next morning, and urged her not to count too heavily on ever hearing from the man again, and reminding her that he had not, they realized after he had left, told them his name or what business had brought him west. Ellen said she had already decided to forget him, and would give her father the dollar the very next time that he came to the post, and so the incident was all but forgotten.

The summer passed quickly, and with the fall, the traders from the west came. Great wagon loads of supplies for the Inn arrived, and everyone was very busy. Violet and Joseph were late in making their visit to the post. Nearly all the regular traders had come and gone, and Emmie was beginning to become concerned about them when they finally arrived. Just two rooms were completely furnished and ready at the new Inn, and they had not planned to be open for business until spring, but Emmie thought it a fine idea to have Violet and Joseph as their first guests, and so they were put up in the new building. Violet was speechless at the sight of the furnishings, and at Emmie's beautiful home. Of course Joseph had told her all about the post, and much she remembered from Emmie's tales of long ago. Even so, it was hard for her to comprehend all her surroundings and when they joined Emmie and Luke for breakfast the following morning, Emmie could tell at a glance that the night had held very little rest for her.

After breakfast, Emmie spent the morning visiting with her sister-like friend, and wanted to hear all about her family, and especially about Teka and Little Luke, whom she had helped bring into this world. But Violet seemed only to want to sit and admire Emmie and her surroundings. Finally, Emmie persuaded her to walk to the river, where she would be less distracted, and they sat by the water and chatted for hours, until they heard Ellen's repeated calls to dinner. They joined the others, and Violet was much more relaxed and she ate heartily. The men spent the afternoon packing the supplies that Joseph requested, and Emmie and Violet chose gifts for the children, who were really no longer children, but were now young adults. Teka had asked her mother to bring her a string of beads like those she still wore that Emmie had brought her so long ago, and Emmie chose a piece of material for the to make a dress and apron, and for the boys, they chose a knife for each of them. Violet and Joseph insisted on paying for the items, but Emmie would not hear of it, sending the items to them as gifts. Violet looked much more rested at breakfast the next morning, and Ellen wondered if she might not make a sketch of her before they left, and so while the bundles were being secured for the journey back home, Ellen made a quick sketch of Violet. She did not finish, but professed she had done enough and could complete the picture from memory, and so before the sun was halfway to noon, they bid farewell to their friends and rode toward their mountain.

The winter was a mild one, and there continued to be a few stragglers stopping at the post throughout the season that was usually the slow time for them. Even though Emmie continued to be quite busy, she suggested that perhaps Ellen would like to spend a few weeks at home with her folks. She was very excited about this, and it was decided she would go for the holidays if the weather permitted, and so she worked on her gifts for all of them in her spare time, and through the long evenings. Emmie suggested that she choose some material from the post and make her mother a dress and her father a shirt. She sewed beautifully, and she knew that Maria would be pleased at the results. She pondered long over what to give Jon, and finally decided on one of her sketches, asking Luke to help her choose which one. The final decision was one of two deer near the river at sundown. She had done the picture in water color and had captured the animals and sunset so perfectly that they almost seemed alive. Luke offered to make a frame for the picture as he had for their portrait, and Ellen was most pleased, and knew that Jon would cherish her gift.

They were sorry to see her leave, even though she would be gone only a short time. They had grown so accustomed to having her with them, and had grown to love her as their own, and they knew that their home would have an emptiness about it until she returned.

Emmie had little time to be lonesome as the exceptionally mild weather made it possible to have the few rooms at the new Inn ready, and they were occupied almost every night. Word came that the canal was near completion, and that water would be flowing in it by summer. At least some sections, if not the entire length, would be open to travel. Their Christmas that year was more a day of rest than festivity, and their gifts to each other were more loving than material. Luke had made Emmie a small wooden chest, beautifully polished and lined with soft leather, and she had knit him some mittens and a scarf from some woolen yarn she had purchased from a traveller who was in need of some supplies. Working with the yarn had recalled to her memory the fire and Ma, but that sad episode in her life seemed a hundred years ago, so far from today and the life she so enjoyed now that it seemed almost as though it had all happened to some other person, and that she had not really been a part of it.

Chapter XVIII

On the same day that Ellen returned, a rider brought a letter from New York City for her. It was from a Mr. Wilson, whom they shortly concluded was the gentleman who had purchased her sketch. They were all so excited that no one made any move to open or read it for several minutes. Finally, calmed enough to do so, they found, upon reading the contents, that he had many orders for her sketches, and would arrive about May 1st to discuss the details with her. Ellen was so very excited that Emmie made her lie down and she prepared the supper that evening. But from then on, Ellen's every spare moment was taken up with talk of Mr. Wilson, and Emmie and Luke grew very concerned for her health and well being, and hoped sincerely that Mr. Wilson's visit would be beneficial, and not detrimental for her. True to his message, he arrived, and he spent hours going over the literally hundreds of pictures that Ellen had done through the years. When he had finally made his decisions, Luke made a rough wooden case for him to carry the pictures in, back to the city. Ellen left the financial arrangements up to Luke and Emmie, Emmie making all the final decisions, and after long hours of discussions and figuring, he finally offered two hundred dollars for the lot he had chosen. Emmie hoped her surpise and amazement did not show or give her away, as she hesitated before accepting the offer for Ellen. Before he left, he asked if it would be possible for Ellen to travel to New York City in the fall, explaining that if the artist was able to be present, he could arrange an exhibit, and that it was possible that she could sell her work for an even higher price. But Emmie said this would not be a matter for her to decide, as Ellen had really only been loaned to them, and he would have to take up that proposition with her parents. And so he was off with a promise to return before the summer had passed.

Chapter XIX

The Inn was ready, and Emmie quickly realized that they needed more help. Between the Inn and the post they had little or no time to enjoy their home or to be by themselves, and Ellen was neglecting her painting. Reliable help was not readily available here in this western outpost. There were many travellers, but all were seeking their fortunes beyond, and they knew of no one reliable that they could hire until one day, late in the summer, a small group of canal workers stopped at the post.

They had a few skins of poor quality, which they wanted to trade for some staples. There were, Emmie gathered quickly from observing the group, two families, and so, while Luke was striking a bargain with the men folk, she engaged the women in light conversation, and quickly found that the mens' work on the canal had been finished. They were hoping to be able to return to Albany, where they could find some work and cheap lodging until they could get themselves established. There were two men, two women and three children. The children were too small to be of much help, but the women and men were an answer to her prayers. Without even consulting Luke, she offered them jobs. Everyone was amazed — Luke most of all, but he knew from the expression on her face, that Emmie knew what she was about. She quickly outlined some duties which were mostly for the women, but she was sure that he could use some help, both here at the post and at the Inn. And so, nearly as spontaneously as Emmie had made the offer, the travellers accepted it. They were all housed temporarily at the Inn in a large rear room that as yet had not been designated for anything special. Luke had originally planned it for a dining room, but the travel so far had not commanded anything so elaborate.

    The families were both Irish; O'Donnell and O'Neil, and they were soon established in the large room. Emmie knew that other arrangements would have to be made if the families stayed, but they all seemed happy, congenial and most grateful at given the opportunity to work for their keep. Emmie and Luke talked well into the night about what could be done, and what chores could be designated to the new-found help.

The whole place seemed overcome with mass confusion the next few days, with more furnishings for the Inn arriving, and everyone trying to help everybody else. The end result was that nothing seemed to be getting accomplished, except for Ellen, who could be found by the river, sketching almost any hour of the day. So Emmie invited everyone to meet at the post after the evening meal, and make some more constructive plans than they had been able to work out so far. She cornered Luke after the noon meal and told him of her ideas, and he readily agreed. There was a small clearing about a mile east of the post that they had made claim to two summers before. They had no immediate plans for it, but it was a lovely spot, and Emmie often rode there to think and relax when business was slow. This land could be worked by the men, if they were willing, and there was lots of time to put in a planting of vegetables for late fall, and they could also build a cabin, and this would solve the problem of lodging, for surely they were cramped in the room at the Inn. The proposition was offered to the O'Donnell's and O'Neils. They were all eager to accept, and so the groundwork was laid for a cabin and a small farm. They decided to move to the land at once, the men constructing lean-tos of boughs to protect them from the weather until the ground was planted, and they could start work on the cabin. The women took turns coming to the Inn each morning and helping with the chores, and life at the post soon calmed down and returned to normal.

There were a few boats on the canal, but there were

only short stretches of the canal ready, and these boats carried only supplies to the workers.

It was in the spring of 1826 and the boats were already plentiful on the canal waters. The canal had opened its full length to travel in the fall of the previous year, and they had all gathered at the lock below the post when cannons had sounded from west to east, from Buffalo to the New York Battery, signifying the opening. The two older O'Donnell and O'Neil children, now four in number, had taken turns keeping a vigil at the lock to alert everyone when the Governor's boat was sighted. When the boat finally made its appearance and passed through the lock, everyone had gathered to meet it and to shake hands with the Governor, an event none would ever forget.

The O'Donnell and the O'Neil men had made a tremendous success of the little farm, and now supplied all the vegetables for the Inn dining room, which was operated by the O'Donnell and O'Neil women.

Emmie was rocking on the new verandah that Luke had added to the front of the post, enjoying the warm spring air. In the house her dearest friend, Maria, was helping Ellen pack in preparation for her trip to New York City. Ellen was a successful artist of quite some renown, and had just last night wed her Mr. Wilson, the man who had discovered and promoted her work. He had finally, with much perserverance, won her heart, and was at long last taking her to the city to live. Luke and Mr. Wilson joined her, and before long Maria and Ellen were ready, and they all walked to the lock to await the packet that would carry the happy couple on their way. Ellen looked so beautiful and grown-up in her new traveling suit, that it was hard for Emmie to remember the young girl that had so eagerly baked cookies and bread in the great oven of the then new iron stove.

The three that returned to the post after seeing the newly-weds off, returned in silence, but their hearts were bursting with happiness. Their dreams had all come true, and they were, all three of them, in just the prime of their lives, with all the wonderful events that they had experienced, and all they had accomplished, and with the great and many changes that they had seen come to pass in the world around them, what could the future possibly hold in store for them?